Cookie Crumble and Murder

Holly Holmes cozy culinary mysteries

K.E. O'Connor

K.E. O'Connor Books

COOKIE CRUMBLE AND MURDER

First edition. April 2024

ISBN: 978-1-915378-77-4

Cover design: www.stunningbookcovers.com

Chapter 1

"Why are they choosing stale scones and weak tea over what we're offering?" I kissed the top of Meatball's fluffy, tan head as I held him in my arms. We watched the queue grow longer as people waited to be served at Brittany Welling's bland Café Costel.

"Woof!" Meatball, my adorable corgi cross, also disliked our competition. We agreed about everything and did everything together. Well, apart from serving the customers in my own adorable vintage-themed café. I had to obey health and safety rules, or I'd get closed down.

I glanced over my shoulder at my almost empty café. If things didn't turn around soon, I'd have to close, anyway.

Another group of tourists, back from visiting the beautiful Audley Castle just up the road, scurried past. They barely gave my pink and white building a glance. All they saw was the familiar logo of the chain café and knew what they'd get by going there.

Disappointment and second-rate cake.

I let out a gentle sigh. I didn't blame them. People were comfortable with the familiar. But my café was incredible. I'd opened it in Audley St. Mary nine months ago. I'd been making a profit, admittedly, a small one, but it was there and slowly growing. My café had become a community hub for the welcoming village residents. Which was why I was shocked when the council approved another café. An off-the-peg, nothing special, chain café.

Meatball whined and licked the underside of my chin as if sensing my growing annoyance.

"I know. I'm worrying about nothing. I just wish that queue was over here." I gave him another kiss. "Let's get you back in your kennel, and then I'll see if anyone needs a refill." I had no concerns about leaving my café unattended for a moment as I walked along the alleyway and into the storage yard at the back.

It was a safe, quiet village that had a place in my heart, and I had no plans to leave, despite the competition muscling in on my little corner of paradise.

Once Meatball was settled in his luxury, heated kennel, which had cost me a small fortune—but he was worth it—I hurried through the back door and into the kitchen, washed my hands, slid on a clean apron, and headed to the front of the café.

The delicious smell of warm chocolate, honey cake, and freshly brewed coffee made my annoyance fade. As did the sunny smile from Emily Spixworth.

"Holly, I'd love a slice of your cookie crumble cake." Emily tottered to the counter and placed her empty patterned china cup and saucer down. "And more Earl Grey would be lovely."

"Coming right up. The crumble cake is a new recipe." I cut her a generous slice. I got the impression Emily was lonely and used the café for companionship as well as delicious cake.

"It's divine. I don't know how you stay so slender, concocting all these treats."

I grinned as I freshened her cup. "It's why I'm always exercising. I won't cut back on the cake, so I have to burn off the calories."

"What's the latest trend this month?" There was a twinkle in Emily's eyes. She'd most likely seen me experimenting. I'd tried it all. Anything to make sure I could eat cake and not get too plump.

"I'm interested in parkour."

"Oh! Goodness. I saw something about that on the television. Young men jumping off buildings, isn't it?"

I chuckled as I took her money and returned some change. "I'd be a beginner, so no tall buildings for me. It's great for core strength, and it looks fun."

"Gentle gardening is enough for me these days." Emily was taking her order back to her table by the window when the door opened and two tall, broad-shouldered men wearing wraparound sunglasses strode in.

A large, black SUV was parked outside the café, the windows tinted so I couldn't see who was inside. But I'd seen this vehicle around Audley St. Mary plenty of times, so I knew where it had come from.

The taller of the two men, a guy in his mid-forties, clean shaven with dark hair, stopped by the counter. Although I couldn't see the direction of his gaze, I had to assume he was studying the cakes. From the sullen look on his face, he saw nothing he liked.

"Good morning, gentlemen. What can I get you? We have some lovely dark chocolate and cherry scones fresh out of the oven, the cookie crumble cake is made from my own recipe, and my white chocolate blondies are proving popular this week."

The other guy was grinning as I spoke. "It all looks great."

"Thank you. Is the order for anyone special?" My gaze cut to the SUV. The back window had cracked open an inch.

"We'll take two of everything," the sullen guy said.

"Is that to eat in?"

"Do I look like I eat cake?"

"Um ... no? Although you should never deprive yourself."

"It's to go."

I pursed my lips. "I'll get a box. Would you like a tea or coffee while you're waiting?"

The shorter guy looked like he was about to say yes, but a quick glance from his companion silenced him. "We don't have time. Just the cakes. Thanks."

My three loyal customers watched with interest. Everyone in the village paid close attention to the Audley family. They'd owned Audley Castle for hundreds of years, passing it along to the next generation when it was time. It was a stunning place, and I visited it several times a month.

The castle was an early seventeenth-century Jacobean building with striking stone cladding. It had over a hundred rooms, and a huge number of staff to look after the place. The current Audley family permitted year-round visits from tourists, who loved exploring the stunning grounds and rooms that were open for public viewing.

The family members were supportive patrons of the village, and would often help local businesses, including buying treats from my café. Although I'd yet to figure out which member of the Audley family sent their security detail here so they could indulge in my treats.

If only the gossip mill would turn fast enough to let people know I catered for such a noble and well-respected family. It would get a few more seats filled.

"Not many people in today," the chattier security guy said.

"It's because of that dreadful new place." Emily wandered over, her eyes bright with interest. "Have you seen the queue? They should be ashamed of themselves, visiting that place instead of coming to Holly's charming café."

"The cake is cheaper," the grumpy security agent said.

"Cheap and mass produced," I said. "Have you eaten in one of those chain cafés? It's all the same. You won't get handmade white chocolate brownies or dark chocolate scones still warm from the oven. Or they'd only be warm because they'd been tossed in the microwave."

The surly agent simply shrugged.

"I'll always stay loyal to you," Emily said. "Although ... the café over the road has a fifty percent off promotion on their brownies. Even I was tempted by that offer. Not that I'd ever go there."

I gulped. I'd barely break even if I offered such a big discount. But Emily was a regular, and I couldn't afford to lose her. "I'll match that deal."

She smiled and clasped her hands together. "How wonderful. I'll take all your brownies for that price."

"Except the two we're buying," the grumpy agent said.

Emily stepped back. "Of course. Which member of the Audley family are you protecting today, Mr. Milligan?"

Mr. Milligan. So that was Grumpy's real name.

His face remained impassive. "It doesn't matter. They're all important."

"I'll give you a hint. The one we're looking after loves cake and feather boas." The other agent nodded at me. "I'm sorry this place is so quiet. Those idiots queuing don't know what they're missing. Even the smell makes me drool."

"No drooling," Mr. Milligan snapped. "Go check the SUV."

"It's fine. All secure."

I placed their boxed order to one side, filled another box for Emily, and took her money. "Don't eat them all at once."

"Thank you, dear. What a treat." She whipped out of the café so quickly she took me by surprise. I'd never seen her move so hastily.

"You've been conned," Mr. Milligan said.

"You've lost me." I grabbed another box and continued filling it with their order.

"That brownie deal ended yesterday. The old girl got one over on you."

I huffed out a breath and placed their order on the counter. "Emily must have made a mistake. She'd never cheat me. Besides, she comes in almost every day. I need loyal, regular customers like that."

"You don't if they cheat you, or you'll soon go out of business."

"That may happen, anyway," I muttered.

The door opened again, and a glimpse of my visitor made my stomach tighten.

Both security agents turned and watched as Brittany Welling dashed to the counter, her long blonde hair tied off her face and a big smile on her glossy pink lips. She wasn't fooling me with that smile. Brittany was as fake as the alleged real chocolate croissants she served in that hateful café.

"Holly! Doesn't your display look beautiful? All those cakes sitting there waiting to be eaten. My, my! You're charging that much for an almond croissant?" Brittany tutted and shook her head. "No wonder you've sold none."

"I've sold two." I shuffled the croissants around with a pair of tongs. "We don't all have the luxury of a head office bulk buying and freezing the goods."

Her bottom lip jutted out, although her gaze was on the security agents. "It's so hard to make a go of a small business these days."

"As I'm discovering since you moved here."

"Oh, hush. I'm healthy competition. And I just saw someone leave with a box of cakes, so you can't be doing that badly. And look, you've got another big order from these handsome men." She winked at the security agents.

Mr. Milligan didn't respond. The other agent smiled, looking uncomfortable as if he knew he was in the middle of a discussion that teetered toward unfriendly.

"Gentlemen, you get free coffee refills at my place," Brittany said. "It's an unlimited offer with a saver card. I just need your contact details."

I rested my hands on the counter. "There are lines you don't cross. One of them is don't poach my customers."

"Holly! We're all friends. And with so many tourists visiting this quaint little place, you get your fair share. It's not nice to be greedy."

My eyes narrowed. "Was there something you wanted? Or did you come in to complain about my prices?"

She giggled. "I'm so absent-minded. I need change, and I can't leave the café with just one assistant, or we'll get overrun with caffeine and cake-starved tourists. I saw you go to the bank this morning. Can you change this for me?" She dumped a pile of notes on the counter. "I'm out of almost all coins. I wish people would realize cards are simpler, but you know how the oldies like to count out their change."

As tempted as I was to tell her exactly where to stick her money, my instinct was to help. There was nothing worse than getting stuck with no change and irritated customers.

"Pretty please. I'll return the favor the next time you run short. Us girls must look out for each other." She fluttered her lashes at me.

Mr. Milligan snorted, but when I looked at him, his face was a blank canvas.

"Let me finish serving here, and I'll see what I've got."

She tossed me an air kiss. "You're an angel."

I wish I wasn't. Sometimes, I wish I had a devilish streak. Then I'd tell Brittany and her pile of moldy brownies where to go. I finished boxing the goodies for the security agents and handed them over.

Mr. Milligan gave me some money.

I checked the notes and passed two back. "You've given me too much."

"Call it a tip." He picked up the boxes, and they walked out.

I watched Mr. Milligan as he presented the cake boxes to the mystery member of the Audley family then tucked the money into the register and glanced at Brittany, who was inspecting her nails and humming under her breath.

Quality always won out. Brittany's café was a novelty, and with more promotion and a few more deals for the tourists, I'd make this work.

I had to. Because if I didn't, I had no idea what I'd do next.

Chapter 2

I set the closed sign in the café window at four in the afternoon the next day. I usually stayed open until at least six-thirty to catch commuters returning home, but today was a special day.

I checked my reflection in the mirror and gave a nod of approval. My dark hair was smooth, I had no streaks of flour on my cheeks, my usual apron was hung up, and I wore a pretty blue and white tea dress.

"What do you think, Meatball? Suitable for royalty?" I curtseyed for him.

"Woof, woof." He wagged his stubby tail in approval.

Two woofs from Meatball always meant yes. At least, that's what I believed.

I crouched in front of him and ran my hands over his soft tan and white fur. Even he'd had a brush for this special occasion.

I picked up my purse, grabbed my keys, secured Meatball's leash to his collar, and we headed out the back door and along the alleyway.

As soon as we stepped onto the street, a whoosh of anticipation hit me, and as we grew near the village green, more and more people appeared, the air alive with excited chatter and laughter.

Flags and bunting fluttered in the pleasant afternoon breeze, and a large marquee was set to one side, with tables covered in food and drink I'd enjoy sampling after the official speeches.

Speeches to celebrate a prince becoming a lord.

"He's so handsome, and I'm sure he looked at me. He's not married, so I have a chance." A woman rushed past with her friend.

"Prince Rupert won't have eyes for you. Princes don't marry commoners. He'll marry a lady."

"That's Lord Rupert to you, and he definitely looked at me." The woman giggled as she dashed past, tugging her friend by the hand as they headed to the stage set on the village green.

Prince Rupert Audley was the dashing bachelor of the Audley family. He was a few years older than me, tall, with messy blond hair and the bright blue eyes all members of the Audley family had. I'd never spoken to him, but I'd seen him in the village. He often had his head stuck in a book. I liked a man who read.

And today, Prince Rupert was hosting a celebration. He'd become a lord after being nominated by the Prime Minister. Prince Rupert was the patron of several charities, and had spent time abroad helping set up twenty water purifying stations. His services to the public had been noted, and as a result, he'd received his new title from the Queen at an event held at Buckingham Palace.

It had been in all the papers, local and national. Our local paper used it as their front cover story for a month!

I was pleased Prince Rupert had brought a celebratory event to the village, rather than hosting it in a fancy, big-city hotel or exclusive venue. The family was true to its roots, and I felt a tingle of pleasure at living in such a wonderful place.

In truth, I didn't understand all the official titles, but it was important to the Audley family, and they wanted to share their success with everyone here. We'd all been sent a gold-embossed invitation to the celebration, and I considered it a treat to be included.

I wanted to get a spot at the front of the crowd but had left it too late and didn't want to squash through and risk Meatball being trodden on. So, we stood back and observed as everyone settled into place.

"Holly! You tore yourself away from those delicious cakes for five minutes to join in the fun." Betsy Malone bustled up beside me, her broad face red and a huge straw hat covered in dried flowers balanced on her head.

"I wouldn't miss this. Did the family let all the staff out of the castle to attend?"

Betsy nodded. "We've got the afternoon off. I had my team working from dawn, so we wouldn't get behind on the housekeeping. That castle doesn't clean itself, and I'm certain there's a secret dust factory somewhere inside those walls. Every morning, there's always more to clean." She pursed her lips, but from the many conversations I'd had with Betsy, she loved looking after the castle and keeping everything spick-and-span. And she'd worked there for two decades, so she had to enjoy her job.

"It's kind of the family to let you all join in," I said.

"They're good like that. Not like some of these snooty families you read about. The Audley family has class." She pointed at the crowd. "And everyone's here. Mayor Baxter's up front shaking hands with everyone. Vicar Liskard has been doing the rounds, too. He's holding a special service later at the church to celebrate Prince Rupert's new title. Oh, look. Even Johnny's made an appearance. Poor man. He's barely left the house these past few weeks. Not since the funeral."

I was taking it all in, but my gaze settled on Johnny Reynolds. His wife's funeral had been held at the church three weeks ago, and I'd catered for the wake. "It's good to see him out. How's he doing since he lost Sally?"

"Well, I don't like to gossip," Betsy leaned closer, "but I've heard things are tough. He hasn't been back to work and has been seen at the pub most nights. He's struggling. Hardly a surprise. Sally was no age. Taken in the blink of an eye by an aneurism. Such a shame."

Johnny's shirt was crumpled and his shoulders slumped as he stood at the edge of the crowd. His gaze kept flicking around, and his hands were clenched. He seemed angry. It must be the grief. It affected people in different ways. Perhaps he thought it inappropriate people were enjoying themselves, when he was lost in such misery.

I'd make him a care package of treats when I got the chance and make sure he knew people were thinking about him.

"I don't suppose there are any of your delicious cakes at this party," Betsy said. "I keep telling Chef Heston about your café. Not that he listens. His loss."

"I'd have loved to cater for today's event, but I know the castle has an excellent team in place. I heard your chef trained in Paris."

"Don't get me wrong, Chef Heston knows his way around the kitchen, but your cakes are better. Don't tell him I said that." She nudged me with her elbow and winked. "He'd bite my head off if he overheard me saying anything bad about his food. That man has too much pride."

"I've eaten his cakes at the castle café. They're amazing." Although maybe not as good as mine, but I kept that thought to myself.

"Oooh! Look! There's Rupert. He's about to make a speech." Betsy stood on her tiptoes. "He's such a nervy young fellow. I hope he doesn't trip over his own feet."

Lord Rupert stepped onto the small temporary stage, which was set with a podium and microphone. He cleared his throat several times, and the microphone whined.

He tapped it and smiled self-consciously. "Good afternoon, ladies and gentlemen. I'm pleased you could take the time to enjoy this celebration. I didn't want to make a fuss over becoming a lord, but my family thought it was the right thing to do." He glanced at his sister, Princess Alice Audley. She wore a beautiful pale blue silk gown, her blonde curls piled on her head. She gestured for him to keep going and rolled her eyes when he hesitated. Perhaps it had been her idea to have this party.

Lord Rupert shuffled a slip of paper from his pocket, smoothed it out, and nodded at the crowd.

As I listened while he spoke about his work with the charity and what happened when he received his nomination, my gaze went to the rest of the family. His sister was there, along with the Duke and Duchess Audley. They were his aunt and uncle, and from what I'd heard about the family, Lord Rupert had grown up at the castle with his sister while their parents traveled.

Next to the Duke and Duchess was a regal, older lady. That was Lady Philippa Audley. She had a huge black feather boa wrapped around her neck, and diamonds sparkled on her earlobes. There was also a plump, grumpy, ancient corgi sitting beside her.

My cheeks flushed when Lady Philippa's gaze caught mine. She gave me a small finger wave and grinned.

She couldn't be looking at me. The Audleys were so far beyond my simple life, I'd never register in their world.

I had no problem with the simple life I'd created, though. I was content with my business, my adorable dog, and my little apartment above the café. Life in Audley St. Mary was perfect, and I was happy.

Lady Philippa waved again, and I slowly raised a hand in acknowledgment. Or should I curtsy?

I settled for a smile and a nod.

My gaze settled on Brittany, who'd wedged herself at the front of the crowd, and my smile faded. Everything was almost perfect. I still had a pile of unpaid bills waiting for me at the café and no idea how I'd beat my rival.

"That's enough of me waffling. Help yourself to the food and drink in the marquee. And have an enjoyable afternoon. Thank you all again for coming today." Lord

Rupert stepped away from the microphone, and his speech was followed by polite applause. He walked back to his family, and I was surprised to see they were staying, rather than getting into their SUVs and returning to the castle.

Since I was at the back of the crowd, I swiftly gained access to the marquee and had my pick of the food. Servers were popping champagne corks and passing out white china plates.

After collecting a plate, I made my way to the dessert table. Meatball behaved impeccably and remained by my heel, even though the enticing smells must have been a challenge.

I stopped by the trays of mini sponge cakes and brownies and gave them my critical appraisal. I hadn't been trained in Paris and didn't go to a fancy college, but I'd served my time at a respectable catering college and loved experimenting with old recipes. Being self-taught was the best way to teach yourself. Well, it worked for me.

I wrinkled my nose at the sunken brownies. "They should have had more baking powder. Or maybe they were over-mixed."

"You're suggesting there's something wrong?" A tall, thin man with a long nose and dark eyes glared at me from the other side of the table.

"Oh! No, I'm sure they're delicious, but I was wondering if something was missed from the recipe. You see how they've sunken in the middle?"

"Holly! Chef Heston knows what he's doing when making a brownie." Brittany appeared by my side, a sickly sweet smile on her face that was directed at the man.

"Chef Heston?" The blood drained from my face. "You're the head chef at Audley Castle?"

"Yes. And your friend is correct. I know how to make a brownie."

"Forgive Holly. She's a perfectionist with cakes. I'm always telling her, if she cut back on using the finest ingredients, she'd sell more cakes and maximize her profits. As a business professional with a thriving café, I always help the amateurs stay afloat." Brittany extended a hand to Chef Heston. "I'm Brittany Welling. I run the most successful café in the village."

"You don't," Chef Heston said. "I do. My café sells out of produce daily."

I pressed my lips together. Chef Heston was blunt, but I had to agree with him. I'd eaten at the castle many times, and the food was always excellent.

Brittany lowered her hand, a flush drifting up her neck and on to her cheeks. "Of course. I didn't mean the castle café. Nothing compares to your food. I was simply saying I run a successful business. Perhaps I could provide a line of treats for the castle. We could work together."

"We make everything fresh on the day. I know about chain café methods. Substandard frozen cakes that have been sitting around for weeks aren't what my customers expect."

"I'd never provide substandard treats." A dark blush colored Brittany's cheeks, shining through the heavy foundation and powder. "You only have to see the queue at my door every day to know I provide excellent quality."

"Or cheap cake and free refills," I muttered under my breath.

Brittany appeared not to have heard, but Chef Heston smirked. "My customers insist on the best, and that's what I give them." He glared at his brownies. "Perhaps something was missed out of these." He whisked the tray away before I tried one.

"You've made Chef Heston angry." Brittany turned on me. "I've been working to get my foot in the door at the castle ever since I arrived in this backward place. I'd make a fortune if I got a line in his café. Tourists always pay more for the food served there."

I wrinkled my nose again. "Good luck with that."

She rapid-tapped my arm. "I'll get there. I never give up when I want something."

"Brittany, you're here."

I turned to discover Donald Barclay behind us, dressed in a smart black suit and tie.

Brittany's smile turned sultry. "Of course, darling. I wouldn't miss this event."

I raised my eyebrows. I didn't realize Brittany was so friendly with our local undertaker.

He rolled his eyes. "Holly, I need to talk to you about your bill for the Reynolds wake."

"I didn't know you catered wakes," Brittany said to me. "Donald, I can do that. And I know exactly what you like." She rested a hand on his arm.

He ignored her. "Is there any chance you could reduce the final bill? Funerals aren't cheap. The headstone costs a fortune, then there's the engraving, and even the coffins have gone up in price recently. And don't get me started on the price of buying a plot. I want to give the best deal to my customers."

"Oh, of course. I'll look and see if I made any errors." I didn't enjoy catering wakes, but needs must. I never put much of a markup on them, because I hated taking money from grieving people.

"I wouldn't normally ask, but Mr. Reynolds is struggling financially, so I wanted to take the heat off him in any way I can."

"Come to me next time. I'll do you a deal." Brittany stepped closer to Donald.

He continued to ignore her, although his clenched jaw suggested her attentions weren't welcome. "Going forward, I may not use your catering. Unless you can considerably cut your fee, it's just not viable."

I chewed on my bottom lip. Losing that money was a problem. I couldn't survive on the café income alone.

"Let me see what I can do. Maybe I could make a basic sandwich spread and cookies. Something more affordable for everyone."

"I'm sure you'll figure things out."

Brittany slid her hand around Donald's elbow. "Shall we go somewhere to talk?"

"Let me go." He spoke through gritted teeth.

A tiny squeak popped out of her lips. "You can't keep ignoring me. I'm here now, and I'm going nowhere. This pretending I don't exist act is tired."

"I didn't know you knew each other." I also didn't miss the tension between them or the way Brittany clutched Donald's arm like he was her favorite slice of cookie crumble dessert.

"Holly, if you'll excuse me." Donald led Brittany to a corner of the marquee and spoke to her rapidly, his head close to hers and fury in his eyes.

While I watched them bicker, another man marched over to join them. I didn't recognize him, so he wasn't a local. Audley St. Mary was so small, everyone knew everyone. But whoever he was, he was also unhappy. The small group wore scowls as they talked.

"Something caught your attention?"

I jumped and looked around to see Mr. Milligan behind me in his usual sunglasses, wearing the same sullen expression. "I was curious about a conversation going on, that's all."

"Curiosity is a dangerous trait to cultivate. Stick to baking." He strode away and hovered close to Princess Alice, who talked effusively with her brother as she waved her hands around.

Meatball whined and nudged my leg with his nose. He looked at the exit.

"Good idea. Let's get out of here, shall we?" The news from Donald about the invoice meant my appetite had gone, and it took a lot to put me off my food.

We snuck out of the marquee while no one was looking and headed to the café.

I needed something to cheer myself up, and I could always find happiness at the bottom of a cake tin. It was time to do what I did best. Get my apron on and whisk up treats.

The bills would still be there in the morning, and I'd fix them then.

Chapter 3

I'd been able to count the number of customers I'd had on both hands since my mini lunchtime rush quieted down. There was always a lull mid-afternoon, but it hadn't been this quiet for a long time, and there wasn't a single person in the café.

I stared at my lovingly prepared brownies and cookies, and my heart gave a sad little thump. It wouldn't be long before I'd be closing the door on my dream forever if I didn't figure out how to turn things around fast.

A quick top-up of my tea and a moment to slide a slice of cookie crumble cake onto a plate, and I headed to the backyard. I also had a chew stick in my pocket for Meatball.

He bounced out of his kennel, his tail wagging. I gave him a good scratch behind the ears and then settled on the bench beside his kennel, feeding him his chew while I sipped my tea and enjoyed the sweet, caramel infused crumble cake.

"What should we do, Meatball? I don't have time for a second job."

"Woof!" He didn't like that idea, and neither did I. If I could squeeze in another job, I'd never see him, and a decent night of sleep would become a distant memory.

"Maybe I should try something on social media. Go viral. Isn't that all the rage?"

"Woof, woof, woof!"

"That's not us, is it?" I tapped my fingers against my mug. "Maybe people just need to sample my cake. I could stand outside with a tray of freebies. Once people taste how delicious they are, they won't be able to resist splurging."

Meatball's single bark held a cautious note.

"Well, you come up with something better. Doggy dancing videos? Or you could walk around the village with a sign on your back pointing an arrow to show people where to come for the most delicious cake they'll ever taste. If we don't get this right, there'll be no more meaty chews for you."

He lowered his head.

I gave his rump a hearty pat. "You'll always get your treats. I'll be the one living on the rice and pasta to stretch the budget." I finished my cake. "Let's cut up some cherry almond brownies and white chocolate chip cookies. There'll be another coachload of tourists arriving soon from the castle. I'll entice them in with those."

Meatball returned to his kennel, and I went inside, washed my hands, and was setting out sample trays when Brittany strode past the café. Donald was beside her.

She was almost running in her shiny red heels to keep up with his rapid stride. He was clearly trying to get away, and she had no intention of letting him do so.

Donald stopped abruptly and turned to Brittany. He jabbed a finger in her face. Brittany held her own and got so close to him their toes touched.

I threw a few cookies on a tray and hurried outside. I needed to make sure Brittany was safe. Donald looked furious, and the argument was escalating. I'd never thought of Donald as a violent man, but I didn't know him that well.

They were so occupied with yelling at each other that they didn't notice me lurking with my cookie samples, so it was easy to get within earshot on the pretense of handing out treats.

"How many times do I have to tell you to leave me alone?" Donald continued jabbing his finger in Brittany's face.

"I have rights. You can't pretend I don't exist." Her voice had a high-pitched whine to it.

"Maybe that's my right. I've had enough of you interfering in my life. Didn't you get the hint when I moved? Why follow me?"

"Darling, you're playing hard to get, but it's time it stopped." She tried to stroke his arm, but Donald avoided her touch as if it repulsed him.

"It stopped for me a long time ago." He raked a hand through his hair. "Brittany, this is harassment. If you don't stop bothering me, I'll get the police involved."

I stopped my jaw from dropping open. This was serious. And they had history. A tangled, unhappy history.

"Donald, please, we can sort this out. It doesn't have to be this way."

"I'm done. Leave me alone, or you'll regret it." Donald turned and strode off. Brittany chased after him.

I watched until they were no longer in view and then returned to the café and placed the sample tray on the counter. What was that about? A failed relationship? A business deal gone wrong? Brittany had called him darling, so perhaps they'd dated. She wanted the relationship to continue, but Donald had other ideas. Whatever it was, Donald was furious about the situation, and Brittany wasn't letting go.

The café door opened, and a bedraggled man wearing a crumpled gray suit shuffled in. He was grumbling to himself as he approached the counter.

I recognized him from yesterday's celebration. He'd been the unhappy man talking with Donald and Brittany. Donald seemed to attract disgruntled people.

"Good afternoon. What can I get you?" I gave him my brightest smile, which he received with barely a nod.

"A strong black coffee and a slice of whatever is good." He looked over his shoulder and kept muttering to himself.

"Everything I serve is good. I make it all myself."

He glanced back at me. "Then you pick. Do you serve booze?"

"Oh, no. I don't have a license. It sounds as if you need something to cheer you up. Bad day?" I selected a large slice of maple pecan pie and set it out for him to inspect.

The man scrubbed at his graying mutton-chop whiskers. "That jerk thinks he knows it all. He won't get away with it."

"Who are you talking about?" I poured him a strong mug of black coffee and detected a faint whiff of whiskey drifting off my customer.

"Donald Barclay. He's always upsetting people. I just saw him doing it again. He enjoys it. I'm certain of it. He has no heart."

I placed a napkin on the counter. "How do you know him?"

The man finally focused on me, and his cheeks grew red. "Forget I said anything. I'm just having one of those days." He inspected the pie. "That looks delicious. You made it?"

"That's right. I hope you like it." I held out the card reader for payment. "Do you work with Donald?"

He pursed his lips and then huffed out a breath. "I wouldn't work with that man again for all the money in the world. He can't be trusted."

"Why is that?"

"He's a bad guy. If I were you, I'd ban him from this lovely café. If you don't, he'll only upset you, too."

"Actually, I do business with him. I've recently started catering for the wakes held after the funerals he takes care of."

"Then I pity you. It won't be long before he's asking you to reduce your prices. That's when you know you're in trouble."

"Why does that mean trouble?"

He tapped a finger on the counter. "My advice to you, not that you've asked for it, is to get out of any contract you have as soon as possible. You'll regret it if you don't." He scooped up his mug, napkin, fork, and plate and took a seat by the window.

A tug of worry centered in the pit of my stomach. When Donald had requested I lower my invoice for Sally Reynolds' funeral, he'd said it was because Johnny was struggling with the expense, but was there something else going on? Donald wouldn't cheat me, would he?

"I need coffee!" Brittany burst through the door, her chest heaving and her blonde hair coming loose from its clip.

I resisted the desire to roll my eyes. "Don't you serve coffee at your place?"

"Don't be silly. Not for me to drink. I'm almost running out of supplies for my customers. You always have plenty."

"That's because I order in time and do regular stock checks." I folded clean paper napkins while discreetly checking outside to see if Donald was with Brittany, but it seemed he'd successfully shaken her loose. "You should try it."

"I'm so busy, I barely have time to take a bathroom break, let alone order stock. Be a sweetheart and grab me some from your storeroom. I'll pay, of course." She raised her purse.

I pressed my lips together. Brittany was always doing this. It was time I put my foot down and got comfortable saying no. "Perhaps Donald could help you."

"Donald! What do you know about him?"

"I couldn't help but notice you arguing."

"That! It was nothing. He's a tease. Such a passionate man."

"And how would you know that? Are you dating?"

Her smile slipped from insincere to fake. "Why the interest in my private life? You rarely want to gossip, no matter how nice I am to you."

I repressed a smirk. Her version of nice was different from mine.

A black SUV glided to a stop outside the café. I was so used to seeing the vehicle, it was no longer a surprise, although I still got a flutter of excitement every time I served the Audley family, even if it was via their security team.

"Holly! My coffee!" Brittany rapped her red painted nails on the counter.

"Just a minute. I have important customers arriving."

She turned and stared out of the window. "OMG! Is that who I think it is?"

Mr. Milligan and the same agent he'd been with the last time he visited strode in. They wore immaculate dark suits and wraparound sunglasses, even though it was cloudy outside.

Brittany turned back to me and prodded my arm. "Lucky you. But I still need that coffee. I've got angry customers waiting."

It was tempting to tell her where to go, and it wasn't to get the coffee. Instead, I did the mature thing. "You've been in my storeroom before. Go grab what you need."

"Thanks. I also need straws and napkins. And I'll take a slice of this while I'm out back." Brittany grabbed some cookie crumble cake before I could protest and hurried off as if she owned the place.

I deep breathed until my frustration was under control. I needed words with Brittany about how often she took advantage of me, but that would have to wait until I'd assisted a very important customer.

I nodded at the security agents. "Back so soon? What will it be today?"

Mr. Milligan gave a soft sigh. "Lady Philippa Audley sends her regards and has a request for one of everything this time."

My eyebrows shot up. "How wonderful."

He stared straight ahead. "Lady Philippa also wants to know if you enjoyed the celebration on the village green."

My gaze went past him to the SUV. "Is she inside the car? Does she want to talk to me?"

"You're not to go near her. Lady Philippa is... fragile."

"I won't be a nuisance. And I saw she has a corgi. Perhaps he'd like to make friends with Meatball. Meatball loves other dogs. I think he gets lonely in his kennel. I was considering getting a companion for him, but—"

"Just the cake. We're not here to chat. And I need an answer to Lady Philippa's question, or she'll make me come back and ask again."

From the tight set of Mr. Milligan's shoulders, it was easy to see he didn't want to be here. But I suppose he had no choice other than to follow Lady Philippa's orders.

He could be less sullen, though. There were worse jobs than visiting the best café in the village and indulging in treats. And his sidekick seemed to think so. He was leaning close to the counter and peering over the top of his sunglasses at the cakes.

I turned to the less grumpy agent. "Would you like a cookie sample? On the house."

He grinned and grabbed a piece of cookie off the tray. "Thanks. It's never a burden being sent here with Lady P in the back of the car. Your café is the first place she insists on visiting when we take her out."

"We don't call her Lady P in public," Mr. Milligan muttered.

The other agent cringed and took a bite of the cookie. "Delicious."

"Holly, I can't find the red napkins," Brittany yelled from the storeroom.

"Top of the shelf on the far right," I called back. I raised my eyebrows at the security agents. "Sorry about that."

"Got them! And the straws?"

I gritted my teeth. "Bottom shelf by the empty glasses. Don't take them all."

"Yep. Found them."

"Staffing problem?" Mr. Milligan said.

"More like a rival problem." I huffed out a breath. "Since it seems you're now regular customers of mine, we should formally introduce ourselves. I'm Holly Holmes."

"We know who you are, Miss Holmes," Mr. Milligan said.

I smoothed my hands down my apron. That comment felt loaded with meaning. "And I know your surname, but do you have a first name?"

"Of course."

"Do you want me to guess what it is?" I tilted my head. "Could you be a Martin? Or a Ralph? Maybe a Richard? Dick for short."

The other agent smirked. "He'll never tell you. This guy's an international man of mystery. I'm Saracen. This is Campbell."

Mr. Milligan, Campbell, gave another much louder sigh. "We're also on duty, so let's keep this professional."

"Always do, boss." Saracen grinned at me then finished his cookie.

"Saracen, have as many cookie samples as you like." I didn't include Campbell in that offer. He was the one being surly, while I was simply being friendly.

"Thanks. I've got a sweet tooth. It's my one flaw."

Campbell snorted.

I set out a box to put the cakes in. "In answer to Lady Philippa's question, I enjoyed the celebration. Lord Rupert's speech was interesting. It's amazing how he raises all that money and finds the time to volunteer at the project, too."

"He's a good guy," Saracen said. "He even helped dig trenches to lay the water pipes."

"He didn't mention that in his speech."

"Lord Rupert is a modest guy. He doesn't like to brag."

Campbell cleared his throat. "You left early."

My head jerked his way. "I'm surprised anyone noticed."

"I notice everything. And you've been noticed. Why leave early?"

I hurriedly filled the box and placed it on the counter before pushing the card reader his way. "I just did. I'm not a fan of crowds, and Meatball was getting anxious. I didn't want him trodden on."

"You talk about this Meatball a lot," Campbell said.

"Of course. He's my best friend."

"Your best friend is a dog?"

I lifted my chin. "Is there anything wrong with that? The Duchess has corgis. So does Lady Philippa."

"Dogs are great," Saracen said. "Campbell likes them, too. He just pretends he doesn't because it doesn't suit his image."

"Of being a scary James Bond?"

Saracen roared a laugh, while Campbell appeared frozen to the spot.

"Isn't that what you're trying to be?" I said to Campbell as sweetly as I could. "It's working. You've intimidated me every time we've met."

"Don't tell him that. You'll inflate his ego," Saracen said.

Campbell slapped the card against the reader with such force, I was surprised it didn't snap.

Since I'd already put my foot in it, I decided another foot would do no harm. "I don't like to ask—"

"Then don't." Campbell pocketed his card.

I pressed on. "It's just that my business has been quiet recently. Do you think Lady Philippa would spread the word about how good my cakes are? An endorsement from the Audley family would be amazing for business. It could save me from closing."

"The family remains neutral on matters of this nature." Campbell grabbed the box.

"I'd give her a discount."

He shook his head.

"Sorry, Holly, but it's not our place to tell the family what businesses they should support." Saracen's shrug was apologetic. "I'll tell everyone, though. And everyone knows our cars, so the locals will figure it out for themselves."

A siren wailed in the distance. It grew close fast, and a few seconds later, a police car zoomed past, followed by an ambulance with its lights on.

Campbell and Saracen raced out of the café, and I hurried after them. The vehicles were heading toward St. Mary's church.

Campbell strode a few steps away, talking on his phone. He ended the call and turned to Saracen. "Secure Lady Philippa."

"What's going on?" I said. "Does this have to do with the family? Is someone hurt?"

Campbell didn't acknowledge me. "I'm going to the churchyard."

Saracen nodded and stood outside the SUV, his hands clasped in front of him, all smiles gone.

Campbell jogged away to the church.

"Trouble?" My lone customer shuffled out, licking crumbs off his fingers, a silver hip flask emerging from a suit pocket.

"I think so. Um... if you don't mind, I'm going to close and take a look."

"Fine by me. I'm finished. And an excellent choice of cake. I'm feeling much more cheerful." He wandered off, swigging from the flask.

"Come back any time." I dashed into the café, grabbed my purse, locked the front door, and stopped. I'd forgotten my unwanted rival was raiding my storeroom and eating my cake. I opened the door and stuck my head in. "Brittany! Are you done? I need to go out for five minutes."

She didn't answer.

"Brittany! I'm leaving." I jogged inside and poked my head into the storeroom.

"I'm in the washroom," she called out. "I'll let myself out. I haven't eaten my cake yet."

"You'll be locked in. I have to go."

"I'll go out through the back door. Don't worry about leaving it unlocked. No one will break in. You have nothing worth stealing."

The cheek of the woman. But I had no time to argue, or I'd miss out on what was happening at the church. I hurried out the back, leashed Meatball, and we dashed to St. Mary's.

When I got there, I was surprised to see so many people. It was usually a peaceful place to walk when I had thinking to do, and I rarely saw another person. But there were over fifty people here, and most of them stood around one spot.

Campbell was there, too, talking to a paramedic and a police officer.

I hurried closer to the crowd with Meatball, squeezed through a gap, and looked into an open grave.

Donald Barclay lay inside.

Chapter 4

My knees wobbled and my pulse raced as I stared at the body. Donald was obviously dead. Crushed by a headstone.

"Everybody move. You're contaminating evidence." A police officer hustled us back, and I was glad to no longer stare at the grisly scene. I hadn't been able to pull my eyes away.

Meatball leaned against my leg, sensing my need for support. I reached down and scratched between his ears, taking a moment to gulp in air and get over a wave of dizziness.

"Miss, I need you to move further back." The same police officer stood in front of me.

"Sorry, of course. It's just such a shock." I waved a hand at the open grave. "That's Donald in there."

"We've yet to make a formal identification. Please, move aside and allow us to do our jobs."

"Yes. Right. So sorry." I staggered away, uncertain what to do next.

Several groups stood around, all glancing at the open grave and talking among themselves. I spotted Betsy and hurried over to join her.

"Holly! Can you believe it? Squashed under a headstone. Looked like a bug on a windscreen."

I grimaced. "I saw the police car and ambulance go past the café. Does anyone know what happened?"

Betsy hoisted her ample bosom up by her bra straps. "He was always hanging around graves. Accidents happen."

"Did he fall in and the stone landed on top of him?"

"No one knows. But whatever he did, it's only just happened. They had a paramedic trying to revive him. Of course, they couldn't move the headstone, so couldn't use shock paddles on him. They declared him dead as I got to the graveside." Betsy's eyes widened as her gaze slid over my shoulder. "Detective Inspector Gerald is here! He doesn't get out from behind his desk for anything small."

I turned and saw Detective Inspector Gerald in a heated debate with Campbell.

There were several police officers milling around, ensuring the scene didn't get too trampled by curious onlookers. And the numbers were growing, so they had a job on their hands.

"Why is Audley Castle security team interested in this death?" I turned back to Betsy. "Campbell and Saracen were in my café getting an order for Lady Philippa when they saw the police car. Campbell ran over here like his life depended on it."

"Don't let Chef Heston hear Lady P is ordering from you. He'll burst a blood vessel." Betsy chuckled.

"I'm always happy to serve her. It's an honor." I glanced back at the ongoing argument. "I understand them getting involved if there's a security risk to the family, but what does Donald have to do with the Audleys?"

Betsy leaned close, her eyes bright. "They own the village. It's not called Audley St. Mary's for no reason. That includes the land they built this church on. They lease it on a peppercorn rent to the Church, but ultimately, the family says what goes with this place, including the cemetery."

"I didn't know that."

"Of course, they rarely interfere. They're not all la-de-dah like some of these posh families. But they have influence and were even involved in recruiting Reverend Liskard. He's a charming man, and even his sermons aren't too dull. He does such good work with the older people in the community. A genuine diamond."

"He is. So Donald's death on Audley owned land means what for the family?"

"You can see for yourself. Campbell and his team will be in charge of the investigation. Of course, the local police will hate it. But Detective Inspector Gerald isn't the brightest fellow. He's old school police and does things the slow, stupid way. Campbell is neither of those things. He'll want a fast result."

I looked back at the two men. "Does that mean Campbell will win the argument they're having?"

"I've never seen him lose one yet." Betsy shook her head. "And if it's Audley family business, they'll want this cleared up quickly and discreetly. A body on their land won't be good for their reputation."

"They'll ensure a proper investigation is done, though?" I said. "I wouldn't like Donald's death brushed under a headstone because the family has a reputation to maintain."

Betsy's sparse eyebrows flashed up. "Why the interest in him?"

"I didn't know Donald well, but we'd started working together."

Betsy adjusted her bra straps again. "That's unfortunate. That man didn't get rich because he was kindhearted. You're best out of it. I suppose you've got no choice now, given he's just been squashed flat." She smooshed her hands together.

Meatball barked and tugged on his leash. The leash clip slipped off his collar, and he raced away, chasing something across the cemetery.

"Meatball! Sorry, Betsy, I'd better catch him." I raced after my misbehaving pup. "Hey, come back."

Meatball pounced on the rag he was chasing, shook it, and growled happily, his tail wagging.

I carefully eased it out of his mouth. It was grubby and paint-stained. "You can't play with this. It could be toxic." I shoved it into my pocket.

"What are you doing here, Miss Holmes?"

I tensed as I turned and discovered Campbell looming over me. "I wanted to know what was going on."

"Why?" The menacing looming continued.

I stood my ground. "You chased after the police car and ambulance, so why shouldn't I?"

"Because it's a part of my job. I assume you got a look in the grave like everyone else?"

"I did. What happened to Donald?"

"That's what I'm here to find out."

"You're in charge of the investigation?"

"Why so interested?"

"No interest." My top lip was sweating, even though I had nothing to conceal. "Was it an accident? How did it happen? I heard he's not been dead long. Was there really no way to save him?"

"A huge hunk of stone crushed him. You don't come back from that." Campbell stared down at me, although whether he was looking at me it was impossible to tell thanks to his ever-present sunglasses. "You seem intensely curious about this man's death. Were you close?"

"No! I mean, we'd done business together, but that's it. I just want to make sure everything is done right. It's—"

"Everything will be done right, since I'll be the one doing it. Was your connection to the victim only professional?"

My knees shook again. This felt like an interrogation. Campbell couldn't be considering I had anything to do with Donald's death. We'd been in my café when Donald had been found. Campbell was my alibi!

I gulped down my fears. "It was only a business relationship. Nothing else."

"Are you sure?"

"As sure as I am that Meatball's adorable and always a good boy. But the way you're questioning me suggests this wasn't an accident." I glanced at the open grave. "When I saw Donald under that headstone, I assumed he'd tripped and the stone fell on him. Isn't that the case?"

"Haven't I warned you before about curiosity?"

"I don't remember. And having a questioning mind is an excellent character trait. What happened to Donald?"

Campbell was quiet for an uncomfortable amount of time. I could see my face reflected at me in his sunglasses. "It's too soon to say."

"It was an accident, though?"

"Was it?"

"It must have been. I know everyone in Audley St. Mary, and they're good people. Most are friendly. We get on with each other." My thoughts turned to Brittany and Donald's recent public arguments. Maybe not everyone.

"It only takes one unfriendly individual for something like this to happen."

My mouth felt dry, and I desperately needed a cup of calming tea and a big slice of cake. Seeing a body was stressful. "I... I suppose so. Which means Donald didn't take a tumble into the grave. It makes no sense anyone would do this to him."

"It made sense to someone."

I was finding it hard to breathe. From the way Campbell kept talking, this was no accident. "Someone knocked Donald into that grave and killed him with the headstone?"

"I didn't say that."

"You're thinking it."

"Miss Holmes, since you weren't here to see what happened, and you didn't know Donald well, I suggest you leave. Unless you want me to keep asking questions. If you pick the last option, I'll uncover all your secrets. I doubt you'll like that."

"I don't have secrets. But I'd still like to know what happened to Donald."

"So would I, but I can't do that while I'm dealing with nosy members of the public. Stick to what you're good at. Go bake a cake and leave this alone." Campbell turned and strode back to Detective Inspector Gerald.

I was less than amused by Campbell's brushoff, but I wouldn't interfere in a crime scene, and I definitely wasn't putting myself on the police radar. If someone killed Donald, they'd be looking for suspects.

I made sure Meatball's leash was secure before taking a last look around the cemetery. "Let's head back to the café." I raised a hand to Betsy as I left and walked along the street, my head full of questions.

What a horrible way to die. Of course, there weren't any nice ways to die, but he must have been so scared. Even if it was an accident, he'd have seen that headstone falling toward him, and there'd have been nothing he could have done.

I got to the café and unlocked the front door. There was a note on the counter.

I went out the back. I took coffee, napkins, and straws. The money is by the till. And I want that cookie crumble cake recipe. Delicious x.

Brittany would get that recipe when I was cold and in the ground. She may have stolen most of my customers, but she wasn't getting her hands on my recipes.

I settled Meatball out back with a bowl of water and another chewy treat, washed my hands, and put on my apron.

As mercenary as it sounded, this death would be good for business, and I couldn't miss this opportunity, not with the bill pile growing.

A fresh pot of coffee had just brewed when the first group came in and the gossip began. Within half an hour, the café was full, my cake counter was almost empty, and I'd learned all about the body in the cemetery. And one thing I'd learned in particular was that no one liked Donald.

"Emily, what did you think of Donald?" I kept my voice low, although the café was abuzz with conversation, so no one would overhear us gossiping.

She placed her empty plate on the counter. "I don't like to speak ill of the dead, but he was cheap. I had a great uncle he buried, and I complained several times about the flowers, the poor quality paper the memorial service was printed on, and even the coffin wasn't the one we'd ordered. Donald had an excuse for it all."

"He charged you for things he didn't provide?"

"He did. And I've spoken to several people, and they had similar complaints. Donald cut corners. And I suspect, although I don't know for certain, he kept the money he saved for himself and didn't pass it to his customers. He only gave me a partial refund because I kept complaining. Most people wouldn't do that."

"I'd heard he was wealthy."

"Death is a profitable business, my dear."

I filled an empty tray with dark chocolate muffins. "Why was the churchyard so busy? I usually walk there with Meatball when we want a quiet stroll. I've never seen so many people in there until today."

"There was a service of remembrance being held in the church when Donald was found. The vicar holds it every year. It's a wonderful way to remember lost loved ones."

"Did anyone from the service see what happened to Donald?"

Emily's eyebrows shot up. "I don't think so."

"Who found him?"

"Reverend Liskard. He almost fainted when he came back to the church. He deals with difficult things every week, but finding a body in an empty grave..." Emily shook her head. "And such a terrible way to die. A strange poetic justice, I suppose."

"I'm not sure I get your meaning."

Emily glanced around and leaned closer. "You'll forgive me for saying this, but Donald made money from people's suffering. And if he was cutting corners in his business, perhaps Karma gave that headstone a nudge."

"You think someone pushed it into the grave when Donald was in it?"

"What a thought! You have an overactive imagination." Emily fussed with her empty plate.

I stared at her. No, Emily Spixworth couldn't have done it. She was a tiny, fragile old lady. A gust of wind would knock her off her feet.

"Holly, are you well? You've gone as white as a ghost."

"I just... I mean, you didn't like Donald much, did you?"

"True, but I'd never hurt him." Her small mouth pursed. "And if you want to check my alibi, I was inside the church with fifty people, paying our respects to the dead."

I blinked and shook my head. "Sorry! Of course, I'm sure this was an accident."

The café door slammed open so hard the glass rattled in the frame.

Brittany rushed to the counter, mascara streaked down her cheeks. "Holly, you must help me. The police think I killed Donald."

Chapter 5

Everyone in the café stopped talking and stared at Brittany.

She grabbed my hand and squeezed. "Tell them I was here. They can't believe I killed Donald."

I tried to pull my hand from her grasp, but her false nails dug in. "Brittany, calm down. I'm sure they don't think you killed him."

"They do! They always look to the wife first." She grabbed a napkin off the counter and dabbed her damp cheeks.

"Wife! You and Donald were married?"

"Is everything okay, Holly?" Jenny Delaney and Mavis Bickley edged closer. Those ladies loved to gossip and were honing in on their latest target.

"I'm begging you to support me. I don't know what else to do. And all those questions. I had to get away." Brittany gave a bubbly sob.

I looked around my full café. The cake was almost gone, and it was nearly time to shut. "Everybody, I'm so sorry, but I must close early. If you come back tomorrow, I'll give you twenty percent off your order for the inconvenience."

There was lots of grumbling as people finished their cakes and drinks, but ten minutes later, the café was empty.

I flipped the sign in the door to close and returned to Brittany. She leaned against the counter as she deep breathed. I was worried she might faint.

"Come through to the kitchen. You can tell me everything." There were still a few old ladies from the village lurking outside, and I wouldn't be surprised if they could lip read, so we needed privacy.

Brittany sucked in another deep breath and followed me into the stainless steel kitchen I'd had put in before the café opened. I'd spared no expense in making sure my baking equipment was perfection.

I pulled out a seat next to the tiny table in the corner and eased Brittany into it, then I whipped up hot chocolate and set a plate of biscoff iced cookies in front of her. I settled in the seat opposite her and blew on my hot chocolate, waiting for her to talk.

Brittany sniffed several times. "I don't know where to start."

"Let's begin with you being married to Donald. How long were you together?"

"Almost ten years."

"Were you having problems? I saw you arguing in the street." I picked up a cookie and bit off a chunk.

She wiped her eyes, smearing more mascara across her face. "More than a few. It's why the police are interested in me."

"What were you arguing about?"

"Our relationship! Donald filed for divorce almost a year ago, and I've been fighting to get him back ever since."

"I had no idea. He didn't want to try again?"

"He would have come around. But things have been tense lately. Donald's been arguing with me, and I've been trying to get him to see sense. We were perfect together. He just lost his way. I knew, if I was around more, he'd realize what he was missing."

I wasn't sure about that, given my own tense relationship with Brittany, but I kept my feelings out of this uncomfortable situation.

"Holly, I'm in serious trouble. The police think I was involved, but I was here! Remember, I came in for supplies. You must give me an alibi, so I can clear my name."

The cookie I held hovered halfway to my mouth. I was my rival's alibi for a potential murder. All my problems would vanish if Brittany ended up behind bars.

She blinked her tear-hazed eyes slowly. "I'm innocent. But I'll admit, I was having trouble with Donald. The man was stubborn, and he couldn't see a good thing when it was in front of him. I still loved him, though. And I wasn't the one who filed for a divorce. I wanted the relationship to work, and I was willing to do anything to make sure it did."

I lowered the cookie. I couldn't do it. Brittany was a pain in my behind, and my life would be much easier without her in it, but I wouldn't lie to improve my situation. "I'll tell the police you were here."

She let out a sigh. "Thank you. For a second, you had me worried."

"It won't be a problem. After all, you were here when Campbell and Saracen were in the café getting an order for Lady Philippa. They'll back you up, too."

"Campbell's the tall, dark-haired one who never smiles, isn't he?"

"That's right. He only seems to smirk or frown."

"He was just speaking to me with Detective Inspector Gerald about what happened to Donald."

"Why didn't he provide you with an alibi?"

"Campbell said he couldn't confirm it was me. He only saw me walking into your storeroom and not my face."

"Ah! Well, don't worry." I awkwardly patted the back of her hand. "I'll tell the police and Campbell you were here, and this'll be cleared up. You're innocent, which means a killer is out there. The police must focus on finding whoever it is and not harassing innocent people."

Brittany grabbed a cookie and turned it around in her hands. "I... um... I may have made the situation a bit worse."

"Why? What have you done?"

"Panicked. I hung around the church, not able to believe what was going on, but then that grumpy agent surprised me. He snuck up behind me and questioned me. I was so flustered and upset that I wasn't making much sense."

I leaned forward in my seat. "Did you say something to make Campbell think you were guilty?"

"No! But then Detective Inspector Gerald came over when he heard me yelling."

"You yelled at Campbell?" I'd have loved to have seen his reaction to that.

"I couldn't help myself. He was being annoying and kept repeating the same question. When the two of them started grilling me, it was too much. I ran away and came here."

"Oh, Brittany. That wasn't smart. Running from the police when they're asking you if you murdered your husband makes you look guilty."

She waved the cookie in the air. "I know! But I wasn't thinking straight. I'm in shock after learning what happened to Donald, and then the interrogation pushed me over the edge. I made a mistake. I came here because I needed to make sure you'd help me. You will, won't you?"

A thumping on the front door made me jump. "I said I would. I'll be back in a moment. Drink your hot chocolate." I hurried out of the kitchen, already knowing who'd be at the front door.

Campbell and Detective Inspector Gerald stood outside, both looking furious.

I unlocked the door and opened it.

"We know she's here. She was seen coming inside."
Campbell thrust a thumb over his shoulder to where
Jenny and Emily were lurking.

"If you mean Brittany, then yes, she is. You'd better
come in."

Campbell marched in first, and Detective Inspector
Gerald scuttled in after him. He had a sweaty
forehead and wore an oversized beige trench coat.
Perhaps he was going for the Dick Tracy look, but it
didn't work. The egg stain on one lapel ruined the
effect.

"I'm sorry I ran." Brittany appeared from the
kitchen and stood behind the counter. "But you
weren't listening to me."

"Did you run because you're guilty?" Campbell said.

"No! I was just explaining everything to Holly."
Brittany sobbed for several seconds before getting
herself under control. "I didn't kill my husband. I love
him. I mean, I loved him. I wanted us to be together."

I walked over and put an arm around Brittany's
shoulders. "I understand why you're looking at
Brittany for this murder, but I can confirm her alibi.
She was at the back of my café. She'd almost run out
of coffee, so she dropped in to buy some of mine.
Campbell, you and Saracen must have seen her."

Campbell stood tall, and for the first time since
we'd met, he removed his sunglasses. His eyes were a
cold, hard blue, and they bored into me like a kebab
skewer. "I saw the back of a blonde woman as she
walked away. It could have been anyone."

"I'll walk away again. I have a memorable walk. And
I do glute bridges, so you'll remember my rear view,"
Brittany said.

Campbell's gaze traveled slowly over Brittany, not
in a creepy way, but in a cold, secret agent glare. "That
won't be necessary."

"Brittany was here," I repeated. "She didn't kill
Donald."

Detective Inspector Gerald seemed more interested in what was left on the cake counter than asking questions, so after an irritated sounding sigh, Campbell continued.

"Are the two of you close?"

"No!" I glanced at Brittany. "Well, I wouldn't say close. We're in the same business, so our paths cross."

"Holly's excellent at making cakes," Brittany said. "I wish I had half her talent. Although she probably wishes she had my sales skills. She'd be rolling in cash if that were the case."

I bit my lip and summoned happy thoughts.

"The headstone that killed your husband was heavy," Campbell said. "I doubt you moved it on your own."

"Or at all, since Brittany wasn't in the cemetery killing Donald. She was in the back of my café helping herself to my supplies, as usual."

His mouth twitched. "What I'm suggesting is Brittany didn't work alone when committing this murder."

My mouth dropped open for a second. "You're implicating both of us in Donald's murder? Even though you were talking to me when his body was found."

"We're firming up the exact time of death," Campbell said.

"I heard he'd only just died when he was discovered. That rules me out."

"Who told you that?"

"My source isn't important. My café was open all day, and I was here. My customers will confirm that. As will you and Saracen. Unless you don't believe your own word."

"Holly would never kill anyone," Brittany said. "She's too sweet to be unkind. She doesn't even kill spiders."

"Why would anyone kill a spider? They eat flies and bugs. They're the perfect house guest."

Brittany wrinkled her nose. "You see. She's an angel. I doubt she's ever had a harsh thought in her head."

I slid her a glance. I'd had a few unkind thoughts about Brittany since she'd muscled in on my territory.

Campbell did a thorough visual inspection of the café before glancing at Detective Inspector Gerald. "Do you have questions?"

He pulled himself upright from the examination of the cake counter. "Oh, no. Just don't leave the village, either of you."

"We live here and work here, so there's no chance of that happening," I said.

Brittany raised her hand. "I have a two-week summer break planned next month. I will be able to go, won't I?"

"Provided you're not charged with your husband's murder, you'll be free to go," Campbell said. "We'll need statements from both of you."

"And we're happy to give them," I said. "Anything to clear our names and make sure Donald's killer is found."

He gave me a hard stare, which I returned with equal vigor. I was surprised when Campbell looked away first.

"We'll also run background checks to make sure there is no hidden history or criminal records. Unless there's anything either of you would like to share now."

"I have nothing to hide," I said.

"Same here." Brittany dabbed her nose with a napkin. "All I wanted was my husband back, and now I have nothing." She collapsed into sobs again.

"Unless you have more questions, Brittany is distressed, so it's time you left," I said.

Campbell looked like he wanted to protest then nodded, turned, and marched out. After looking flustered for a second, Detective Inspector Gerald did the same.

Brittany hugged me. "Holly, I can't thank you enough. You've saved me. I was so scared when they were questioning me. I thought they'd put me in handcuffs, and I'd never be seen again. I owe you one."

I eased out of the hug and walked to the door to make sure it was properly shut. "Would you consider closing your café? Then I'd consider the debt repaid in full."

A laugh tinkled out of Brittany. "You are funny. As if I'd ever close my café. It's far too successful. I'm even planning later opening hours."

I forced a chuckle. It was worth a try after getting Brittany off a murder charge. But I'd had my opportunity to get rid of her for good, and instead, I'd done the right thing.

If only I felt better about it. And I had a grim feeling that right thing would return to bite me.

Chapter 6

The grass was damp beneath my feet as I walked Meatball early the next morning. There was a chill in the air, despite the sun rising over the rooftops.

I tugged my jacket tighter around me, my thoughts on Donald, and headed to the cemetery.

Meatball was happy to wander in front of me, sniffing the fascinating scents and marking his territory in the way dogs do.

I paused by the low stone wall surrounding the church and looked at the open grave where Donald's body had been discovered. It was covered with a small white police tent, so I couldn't see anything. I was grateful for that. I still had the distressing image of Donald crushed under that stone etched into my brain.

Although I hadn't been close to Donald, my eyes hazed with tears. I pulled a hankie from my pocket. Instead of finding a pristine white hankie to dab my eyes, I held a grubby, paint-stained rag. Of course, this was the treat Meatball discovered in the cemetery when he'd escaped.

It went back in my pocket, and I found a crumpled hankie and dabbed away my tears. Death was always sad, but from what I was learning about Donald, he'd been unpopular, and there'd be few tears shed over his demise.

Perhaps he'd put someone's nose out of joint by refusing to pay a bill or asking for a reduction, and they'd come after him. Or his death could have been a spur-of-the-moment thing that happened in anger. After all, how could anyone know when a grave would be open to push someone into?

I was worried about Brittany's involvement, though. I was prepared to give her an alibi, but I'd seen her arguing with Donald twice, just before his death. Was there any way she could have killed him and used me as her cover?

I shook my head. When she'd marched into my café demanding supplies, she seemed her usual over-the-top, artificial self. She hadn't been panicked, out of breath, or sweating after shoving her husband into a grave and then hurling an enormous headstone on top of him.

And the timing was an issue, too. She'd have only had moments to murder her husband, get to the café, and act like everything was normal. It would have taken a master criminal to pull off such a deception.

But Brittany was excellent at faking our friendship so she could get what she wanted. How far would she go to get something she desired or to exact revenge on someone who'd wronged her?

That was an unkind thing to consider. It was the worry about the bills I needed to pay that made me cranky. Brittany didn't kill Donald.

And that meant there was a killer in Audley St. Mary, and I wouldn't ignore that unwelcome fact.

I looked over my shoulder, a chill snaking down my spine, but other than a chubby robin and a fat blackbird searching for breakfast among the damp grass, it was just me, Meatball, and the quiet residents buried in the cemetery keeping me company.

I lingered for a few more minutes, my future feeling uncertain. I guess a murder so close to home would make a person feel like that.

"Good morning, Holly. I rarely see you up and about at this time." Reverend Ian Liskard rode up on his bicycle and stopped beside me. His round cheeks were ruddy from the cold. He pushed his glasses up his nose as he smiled at me.

"I couldn't sleep. I kept thinking about this." I pointed to the covered grave.

"Isn't it a terrible business? I was on the phone for several hours last night, talking to the Bishop, the police, and the security agents from Audley Castle. I even spoke to the Duchess. She's such a lovely lady and so understanding. She told me not to worry if services have to be canceled." He shook his head. "But I hate to disrupt the routine. There are so many people who rely on the church, not only for spiritual comfort, but for the sense of community. Especially the older people. It worries me they're sitting home on their own, too scared to come to the church after what happened."

"Woof, woof!" Meatball bounced over to say hello to the vicar.

"Meatball, you know Reverend Liskard is nervous of you," I said. "Be gentle."

Reverend Liskard backed away several steps. "Sorry, he's adorable, but after that incident with the German Shepherd who pushed me into the duck pond, I've always been wary of dogs."

"I can understand that." The story about the vicar getting a dunking by a delinquent dog had made the front page of the local paper not long after I'd arrived in the village. I put Meatball on his leash so he couldn't terrorize Reverend Liskard. "Meatball is a softy. Give him a treat and a belly rub and he'll be your best friend for life."

The vicar's laugh was tinged with nerves. "I'm sure you're right. But when I was in the water, I thought I might drown. It's true what they say. Things flash before your eyes when you're gasping for breath."

I looked at the covered grave again. "Perhaps that happened to Donald, too. He must have been scared in his last few seconds. Trapped with no way out as his killer dragged that stone over to crush him."

"Oh, of course. That was thoughtless of me." He was quiet for a few seconds. "I was five minutes too late to save him. Did you know I found his body?"

"I heard." My smile was apologetic. "You know what the village is like. People gossip, no matter how morbid the subject."

"It's only natural. I don't think badly of anyone for talking about such a shocking event." Reverend Liskard settled his clasped hands in front of him as if he was about to give a sermon. "Once the onlookers were removed from the churchyard, they brought Donald out. I was there when they laid him on the ground."

"That must have been difficult to see."

"I've been around death many times, but it never gets any easier." He rubbed his hands up and down his arms. "I kept looking around while the police did their checks and cordoned everything off, thinking the killer must be close by. I only missed him committing his crime by minutes. If I'd been there sooner..."

"You could have found yourself in danger, too."

He nodded, although I wasn't certain he'd heard me.

"Why did you look at that particular grave?" I said.

Reverend Liskard's nose wriggled. "I know my graves, and something looked wrong with the earth. I've seen hundreds of open graves and stood around plenty more. The earth is always heaped on one side, and I noticed it had been disturbed around the grave I found Donald in."

"Was there a fight between Donald and his attacker before he was pushed in?"

He shuddered. "Perhaps. Are you cold? Shall we go in the church? Margaret will have put the heating on, and we can have tea. Standing here talking about such dark things is giving me the chills."

"Thank you. I'd like that." I'd also been feeling paranoia prickling over me as we'd discussed the murder.

"This way." Reverend Liskard led me along a stone path. He opened the large wooden church door with its large black handle.

It was a small church, with twenty fixed pews that looked onto a simple altar with a beautiful stained glass window at the back depicting Moses. The air smelled of lemon polish, and I got a faint whiff of tea. Although there were electric lights dotted around, there were plenty of large white candles flickering, lighting the dark corners of the church.

Reverend Liskard took me through a small arched door at the back and into a dated but clean kitchen. "I don't know where Margaret is, so I'll pour the tea she's left. I can always rely on her for regular sustenance." He set out two mugs and poured strong, dark tea for me.

I nodded my thanks as I added milk and stirred.

"Since you started catering some of the wakes in the area, I've been enjoying the food. Those tiny fairy cakes with the buttercream filling are divine. I have to watch my gluttony when I'm around your desserts."

"Thank you. It was a new business venture I set up with Donald. I'm not sure I'll continue anymore, given what's happened."

"Oh! You surprise me. Donald wasn't known for extravagance in his business." Reverend Liskard settled in a seat.

"I'm not sure I follow."

"Please don't take this the wrong way, but I only ever visit your café if I wish to indulge. It's the prices, you see. They're too rich for me."

My cheeks heated. "I understand. I always hope people see the quality of my baking and the love, care, and attention I put into the food. That doesn't come cheap."

"I'm sure it doesn't. And the villagers adore your café. It wasn't a criticism. I'd be there every day if I could afford it. Your food is sent from the heavens. I'm certain of it."

"Do you think Donald considered my food too expensive?"

Reverend Liskard tilted his head from side to side. "Donald always had a tight hold on the purse strings of commerce."

"I've heard that mentioned before. He was negotiating with me to lower my last invoice."

"Ah, so you saw his cutthroat side. He had a sharp eye on the bottom line. All Donald cared about was how he could maximize profits. I had to speak to him sternly on several occasions when he used a cheap coffin instead of the one he'd promised the mourners. And I know he passed off cheap coffins as the more expensive ones."

"What did he say when you confronted him?"

"That there was a supply shortage, so he'd had to use a substitute, or the family had asked for a change at the last minute. I wasn't always convinced he was being truthful, though." Reverend Liskard sipped his tea. "And he was often late paying donations to the church for the use of our services. I had to send reminders. Much like you, we provide a valuable service to our community, but I need a small amount of money to ensure I can continue to do so. Donald was the only undertaker I ever had problems with. Everyone else paid promptly."

"That must have made him unpopular if that was how he did business," I said. "Do you think... well, could that be the reason this happened to him?"

"Goodness! I can't imagine why someone would think it acceptable to do such a terrible thing." Reverend Liskard stared out at a large oak tree in the cemetery. "Although you could be right. And of course, that's how the rich stay wealthy. They keep the profits and don't share. Charity and generosity do us good, and it creates a wonderful spirit in a person. You have that spirit."

I blushed under his praise. "I do what I can to help the village."

"You've done more than you realize by coming to Audley St. Mary, Holly. Everyone talks so kindly about you. And they always effuse about your cakes."

"That's kind of you to say. Next time you come in, tea and cake are on me."

"You see, a generous soul."

I sipped my stewed tea. "Did you know Donald was married to Brittany Welling? He was divorcing her. She wasn't happy about it."

"I really couldn't say. I'm not one for gossip."

"I don't like to pry into what happened to Donald, but I'm Brittany's alibi for his murder. The police are still concerned she was involved, though."

He pushed his glasses up his nose and took a gulp of tea. "How stressful for you."

"Do you have an opinion about their relationship? Were they having troubles?"

"That's not for me to say. And anything she confided in me about must be kept in confidence."

I pressed my lips together. Of course, the vicar wouldn't break a confidence, but it sounded like Brittany had secrets she'd been sharing. I wanted to ask more questions but shouldn't intrude on Reverend Liskard's sanctuary or press him to give me information he couldn't divulge.

There had to be another way to find out more about Brittany. I needed to make sure she hadn't taken advantage of me, like she so often did.

"There you are, Vicar." Margaret Monzo bustled into the kitchen.

"Morning, Margaret. Thank you for the tea. Holly and I were having a catch up."

"You're welcome. It's what I'm here for." She patted a large black piece of cloth over her arm. "I've got your cassock to repair. After I'm done with that, I'll clean the candle wax off the floor. Can't have anyone slipping." She looked at me and smiled. "I always have jobs to keep me busy."

Reverend Liskard ducked his head. "I'm sorry about the mess. You know me, clumsy to a fault. I was carrying a bundle of prayer books and wasn't looking where I was going. I got my foot caught and knocked over half a dozen candles."

"Don't you worry. I'll get it cleaned in no time."

"You're an angel sent from heaven, Margaret."

She waved a hand in the air. "I'm happy to do God's work. And speaking of God's work, Johnny's in the church. He could do with a few kind words. He's looking wretched again."

"Of course. I'll be right out to see him." Reverend Liskard stood and finished his tea. "Sorry, Holly, but duty calls."

"I won't hold you up. Thanks for the tea and conversation."

"You're always welcome here." He glanced at me as we walked back into the church. "I don't see you at our services, but I like to talk to a parishioner when I can."

I winced. I had nothing against the church, but I opened the café on Sundays to catch weekend tourists and couldn't afford the time off to go to services.

Reverend Liskard patted my arm. "There's no need to feel uncomfortable. We all have busy lives. But know I'm here for you if you ever need me."

"I do. Thanks again." I hurried along the aisle with Meatball.

Johnny stood at the back of the church, his face pale and his hands clasping a pew. I never knew what to say to someone who'd suffered such a tragic loss, so I settled for an awkward smile as I dashed past.

Once outside, I looked at the covered grave. After my conversation with Reverend Liskard, I had more questions than answers about what happened to Donald and a deep sense of unease there was a killer in this village who needed to be stopped.

I had to hope Campbell and the police knew what they were doing.

Chapter 7

The lunchtime rush had just ended, and I'd collected the plates, glasses, and mugs, placed them in the dishwasher, and settled against the counter with my income and expenditure files open on my laptop and a pile of bills I needed to prioritize next to me.

The red line looked alarmingly red, as if someone had taken a pot of strawberry jelly and tossed it across my screen. I'd checked the figures three times, and that amount of red was correct. I wouldn't make the rent this month on my store if things didn't turn around.

My heart gave a thump that was a combination of panic and sadness. Owning my own café had been a dream since I realized a career as a food historian would never be a reality. I had no regrets about going to university and studying history. I just wish I'd had more guidance as to the career path it would lead me along. Or lack of one.

But my second love was baking, so I was happy doing this. I didn't want to lose my café or the compact, cozy lodgings that came with it. This was the perfect spot for me and Meatball, and I loved Audley St. Mary. Even though I hadn't been here long, it felt like home, a place I could stay for the rest of my life.

But that wouldn't happen if I couldn't figure out how to make the red go into the black.

The café door opened, and I looked up. Uh oh! Campbell was here. And, as usual, he wasn't smiling.

I tucked away my bills and closed my laptop. "Late lunch or early afternoon treat?"

He strode over. "We need to talk."

"If you're here to discuss the latest recipes in *Good Housekeeping*, I'm always open to chat."

"Don't be cute." Campbell gestured to a table far from the remaining customers.

It looked like I had no choice but to talk to him. I poured two mugs of coffee, walked over, and set a mug in front of him.

He glared at it as if it had done something wrong to him then nodded and relaxed a fraction. "Thanks."

"You're welcome. Tough day?"

"You wouldn't believe me if I told you."

"I might. I hear all sorts of odd information working here."

Campbell sighed and rolled his shoulders.

"I have a suggestion. You don't always have to play hardball when you interrogate people. Sometimes, a little sugar works wonders."

"I'll take your word for it." He gestured to the seat opposite him.

I held in my own sigh as I perched on the edge of the seat. I waited for Campbell to talk.

He took his time but finally drew in a breath. "Tell me more about your friendship with Brittany."

"We don't have one." I clasped my hands around my mug. "Brittany pretends to be my friend, but she's using me."

"You let her use you?"

"I... Yes, I suppose I do."

"Do you consider yourself someone who's easily influenced?"

"Absolutely not!"

"So why is Brittany walking all over you?"

I slumped in my seat. "Because I don't know what else to do. My life has gone from amazing to stressful since she opened her café. Everything was going so well for me and Meatball, but I'm struggling to make ends meet. It's all Brittany's fault."

"But you still let her mess you around?"

"I'm working on a plan." I had no clue how to deal with my rival and get my café customers back, but I never admitted defeat.

"You charge a lot for your cake."

I narrowed my eyes. "It's excellent cake. It's not mass produced processed rubbish full of emulsifiers and fake sweeteners. Quality will always win."

"If you served your cake at Audley Castle, you could charge these prices." He pointed at my carefully handwritten chalkboard of delicious treats.

"I have to charge that amount. This is my only source of income."

He sipped his coffee. "This is good."

"Organic and fair trade. Only the best."

Campbell tapped his fingers on the table. "Holly, a word of advice. Not everyone wants the best or is prepared to pay for it. Cheap and cheerful often does the job."

"You're a businessman and a secret agent?"

"Who told you I was a secret agent?"

"It was a joke. Or were you? Is that how the Audley family found you?"

"I'm asking the questions. I'm also giving you unsolicited advice. If you want to stay in business, offer more basic food and affordable options. Not everyone is a muffin snob."

"Neither am I. But I've never baked a basic cake in my life."

"Then do a budget range like the supermarkets. Charge half the price and sell three times as much."

"Anyone can do that. My café would be as bland as Brittany's if I offered the same as everyone else."

"Maybe everyone else is keeping their business afloat." Campbell shrugged. "It's your choice. It's also the customers' choice. Are they really coming here every day to spend so much money, when they can wander across the street and get something edible for half the price?"

I glared into my mug. As if Campbell knew anything about running a successful business. "How about you stick to quizzing me about whether I was involved in Donald's murder? I'd feel more comfortable with that."

"Sure. It sounds as if you weren't friends with Brittany but rivals."

"Business rivals, and I've been struggling to keep up with that rivalry."

"Did you frame Brittany to get rid of your competition?"

My mouth dropped open. "Have you deliberately come here to put me in a bad mood?"

"It's a theory. Brittany's small, and I'm not convinced she's strong enough to push Donald into the grave and drop the headstone on him."

"Which suggests you think I did it because I'm not small." I carried a few extra pounds, but there was no need to point it out. And being a little heavier didn't automatically make me strong enough to kill Donald.

Campbell didn't apologize. "You work out."

"How would you know that?"

"You've been seen around the village. Last month, you were jogging, and a couple of months before that, you were doing tae bo on the village green. That'll get you strong."

"It does. But I don't work out so I'll be fit enough to kill people! You need to move on from involving me in this murder. It would have been impossible for me to be involved."

"You're often seen in the churchyard."

I slapped my hands flat on the table. "Are you spying on me?"

"I watch for any threats to the Audley family."

"I'm a threat?"

"You're a person of interest."

I had no clue what he meant by that. I let out a slow breath. "All I want to do is bake cakes, hang out with my dog, and enjoy a simple life in this village. I'm not complicating things by killing a man I barely knew, nor framing Brittany, no matter how irritating she is to my bottom line."

He tilted his head a fraction. "Things are really that bad?"

"That's my business, not yours."

"Are they?"

I wriggled my toes. "Since you gave me unwanted advice, I'll give you some. Brittany is innocent. Yes, she's annoying and a rival, who I wish had never come to Audley St. Mary, but I don't think she's a killer."

"Maybe not. But she is a stalker."

My mug froze halfway to my mouth. "A what?"

"Brittany isn't as innocent as you think. She only moved here to rekindle her relationship with Donald. He'd had enough and filed for divorce on the grounds of unreasonable behavior. Brittany had been following him because she thought he was seeing another woman. She also put cameras in their house to watch him. The woman became obsessed."

I took a few seconds to mull over this information as I sipped more coffee. "The timeframe still doesn't fit. Donald was killed while Brittany was in my storeroom. I already told you she came in for supplies, and when I left to see what was going on at the church, she was using the bathroom. It wasn't her."

"How do you know exactly when Donald died if you're not involved?"

I pressed my lips together. Oops! I'd just been caught snooping.

"I'm waiting for an answer, Holly. Unless you want me to think you're involved again, I need your source."

"It's hardly a secret. Everyone is talking about what happened to Donald."

"Who was your source?"

"Oh, fine! I got chatting to the vicar. Reverend Liskard invited me in for tea and told me everything he knew. He wanted to unburden."

"Probably after you prodded him with unwelcome questions." Campbell shook his head. "He's almost as nosy as you, though, and was getting in the way when we brought Donald's body out. He said he wanted to help a lost soul on his way. Nothing I could do would dissuade him the lost soul had already wandered off."

"Don't be too hard on the vicar. It must have been a shock to discover Donald. And we weren't gossiping about the murder. He just wanted to talk things through. Talking makes everything better."

"It does for some." Campbell downed his coffee. "That's enough, Holly. Stop poking around in this investigation. It's not a game."

"I can't, since you keep circling back to the belief I'm involved."

"It's my job to be thorough. If I return and ask the same questions to the same people, it's because I need to find out if they're lying or covering for someone else."

"Someone like Brittany?"

"Exactly."

"I know she's the obvious suspect because of her tangled past with Donald—"

"He has a restraining order on her. She was ignoring it."

"Well, that was unfortunate. But I've thought it through, and Brittany didn't have time to commit murder and come to my café looking composed and irritatingly happy. If I ever kill someone—"

"Let's hope it never comes to that."

"Same here, but if I did, I'd be a mess for weeks. I may never recover. And after I'd done it, I'd hide in a dark room for days until I stopped shaking and having flashbacks. Brittany didn't behave any differently to how she normally does. Despite her being obsessed with

Donald, there was no way she could have done it. You're looking in the wrong place."

"My focus remains on her."

I finished my coffee. "You should speak to the man who argued with Donald at Prince Rupert's ceremony."

"Lord Rupert."

"Oh, right. That'll take some getting used to. Anyway, this man came over when Donald was arguing with Brittany. I was paying attention because I'd been chatting to Donald about some business we'd done together."

"Catering for the wakes."

I arched an eyebrow. "You have done your homework."

"It's my job. Go on."

"Donald pulled Brittany away, and they were arguing when this other man joined in. And he came in the café the other day, still angry with Donald. When he learned I'd done business with him, he warned me off and said it was a mistake."

"Interesting. Did you get a name?"

"No, but he knew Donald, so I suspect they'd done business together if he was warning me about doing the same."

"I need a description." Campbell took out a notepad, flipped it open, and clicked the top of his pen.

"He was in his mid-seventies, tired-looking, big mutton chop whiskers streaked with gray. His suit had seen better days. He ordered strong black coffee, and I gave him a slice of maple pecan pie. Then he sat by the window, grumbling to himself."

"He was grumbling about Donald?"

"I couldn't hear. You must have seen him. He was here when you arrived to get the order for Lady Philippa."

"The description rings a bell. It'll be easy to trace Donald's former business associates."

"It would also be sensible to check the man's movements before he came to the café."

"I know how to do my job, Miss Holmes." Campbell tucked away the notepad and stood. "Leave this alone. You've done enough."

"Are you sure you don't want me to stay involved? After all, I just provided a new suspect. You may never have learned about this man's dislike of Donald if it weren't for me." I gave him my sweetest smile, but it was tinged with smugness.

"Stay out of this. You'll only complicate things." He turned and marched out of the café.

I watched him go before picking up our empty mugs and walking behind the counter. I wasn't bowing to Campbell and his intimidation tactics. And I saw no harm in dropping in on Brittany and this mystery man, if I could figure out who he was, with cake, sympathy, and a few questions of my own.

Chapter 8

Once the café was closed and the daily takings banked, I put together a mini hamper of cakes. I'd show Campbell that being nice and serving delicious sugar laden treats got more information than veiled threats and warnings to stay out of other people's business.

And as far as I was concerned, this was my business. I was the prime suspect's alibi. Most regretfully, I'd seen the body, and I'd done business with Donald. That made me involved, even more so when Campbell kept poking a finger at me and suggesting I'd been Brittany's accomplice.

I walked out the back door of the café. "Meatball, let's see what we can find out and prove to Mr. Grumpy Pants cakes aren't the only thing we excel in."

Meatball was always happy to go for a walk, no matter where we were headed. He bounded around, only pausing for a few seconds so I could get his leash clipped on his collar.

With the full basket of goodies over one arm, I walked along the alleyway and onto the main shopping street of Audley St. Mary.

I waved at the other store owners as I walked along. It was such a friendly community, which only made this murder even more shocking. How could Campbell expect me to stay out of this when it had happened so close to home?

My walk to Brittany's small, terraced house on Gunwell Street took me past the churchyard, and I slowed to observe a group of volunteer gardeners tidying the headstones and removing weeds.

"Would you like to join us?"

I jumped as Reverend Liskard's head appeared over the wall. He wore a white hat and green gardener's dungarees.

He chuckled. "Sorry to give you a fright, but there's a vicious thorn bush down here I'm tackling. It's not fair to expect the volunteers to get bloody in the name of churchyard conservation."

I rebalanced the hamper over my arm, gently shushing Meatball as he barked a welcome at the vicar. "It looks like you're having fun."

"We are, but we always need an extra pair of hands if you have free time." His gaze went to the hamper. "You already have plans for the evening?"

"I'm checking in on Brittany. This must be a stressful time for her."

He took off his gardening gloves and tipped his hat so he could wipe his forehead with a hankie. "I can only imagine. I had a visit from the police this afternoon. They're still asking questions, and they've yet to catch the killer."

"I got a visit too, from Audley Castle security. The man who questioned me had the cheek to suggest I was involved."

A burst of laughter shot from Reverend Liskard's lips. "Was he unwell? I couldn't imagine a less likely killer. Although you may give one or two people diabetes with your sugary treats."

"I use the minimal amount of sugar. And I prefer date and coconut sugar as natural sweeteners."

"I'm teasing." His hand went to his stomach. "Although just thinking about your cakes is making me hungry."

"I have plenty, if you'd like one."

He pursed his lips. "I wouldn't say no. Are you sure you don't mind?"

"You're welcome. I brought plenty. Help yourself. I've got cookie crumble cake, biscoff iced buns, and cherry scones. All made today."

"The cookie crumble sounds divine." Reverend Liskard looked into the basket I held out. He selected a slice of crumble cake and took a bite. "Delicious."

"That'll give you an energy boost to get the rest of the thorn bush."

He looked at his feet. "It may be a task beyond me, but I'll persevere. You only fail when you give up trying."

I glanced back at my café. I wasn't giving up on my dream. No matter what it took, I'd make my life here a success. "That's very true."

"And life persists. No matter what I do, I'm sure this bush will be back next year." Reverend Liskard waved his free hand across the cemetery. "And even though death is such a permanent state for those who experience it, the world continues turning. Graves need tending, volunteers need tasks to occupy themselves, the congregation needs looking after, and people need cake from you to feel nourished and happy."

I felt a touch emotional, discussing such a deep topic over cake and thorn bushes. "For those left behind, life goes on."

"It does. Although the grief stricken struggle to accept that, it's the truth. The death of one person is a tiny blip on this marvelous planet." His gaze drifted across the cemetery. "But for some, they remain stuck in grief and see no way forward."

My gaze traveled to where he looked. Johnny kneeled at his wife's grave, his head down and his shoulders hunched. "You have such a tough job. I don't know how you do it."

"Tea, sympathy, kind words, and time. Although I suspect this business with Donald hasn't helped Johnny with his grieving." Reverend Liskard finished his cake. "I'll make sure he's okay."

"Best of luck with the thorn bush." I headed away from the churchyard with Meatball.

Seeing Johnny so grief-stricken and listening to the vicar's words about death and life going on, I realized how easily I'd gotten trapped in my own concerns. Everyone had problems, many much larger than mine. I shouldn't stress over my bills. I'd figure something out.

I arrived at Brittany's red front door and knocked. She opened it a moment later.

"Holly! This is a surprise." She wore leopard print leggings and a matching tunic top, fluffy white boot slippers, and had golden bangles on both wrists.

"I hope you don't mind me dropping by, but I figured you'd need someone to talk to."

"About?"

"Donald!"

"Oh! Well, yes. It has been stressful." Her gaze went to the hamper. "Is that for me?"

"I never visit without bringing treats. Perhaps we could have them with a pot of tea."

Brittany smiled. "You've won me over. And it would be nice to talk to someone who isn't trying to get me to confess to a murder. Come in." She led me along a short hallway and into a large, open-plan living space with a gloss white kitchen at one end. "Sorry, Meatball stays in the hallway. My white carpets aren't made for muddy paws."

Meatball whined as if he understood he was being banished from the gossip and cake.

I led him into the hallway and fed him one of the many dog treats I kept in my pockets. "I won't be long. Be a good boy." I returned to the living room and closed the door on Meatball's sad face as gently as I could.

"Take a seat. The tea won't be a minute." Brittany brought a knife, plates, and napkins.

"I had a visit from Audley Castle security today."
I settled on a crushed gray velvet armchair that
threatened to swallow me it was so soft. "Campbell
Milligan. I thought he might have been over this way
to question you, too."

She tipped her gaze to the ceiling. "Ugh! That man
won't leave me alone. He's obsessed."

I raised my eyebrows. That was a poor choice of
words, given her history with Donald. "Campbell's
gotten things the wrong way around and won't budge.
He even suggested we worked together to murder
Donald."

A bubble of hysterical laughter shot out of Brittany.
"He's clutching at straws. He keeps asking me the
same questions and trying to figure out when I
murdered Donald." She walked over with two mugs
and a pot of tea and set them down. She poured the
drinks, picked two cakes from my hamper, and settled
on the couch opposite me.

"I'm wondering if it's because he has no other leads.
And..." I deliberately left the sentence unfinished.

"Go on. Have people been gossiping? The villagers
can be spiteful under their pearls and sweet smiles.
They're small-minded gossips."

"Oh, no, I didn't mean that." I clasped my hands
together and rested my elbows on my knees. "It's
something Campbell told me. I think he was revealing
information to see if I'd change my story."

"I don't see him as the gossipy type. More silent and
sullen." Brittany pursed her glossy lips.

"It was about your relationship with Donald. He...
err... well, he said you'd been stalking Donald after he
filed for a divorce."

"You can't stalk your husband!"

"I think you can."

"Even if you can, which you can't, Donald was always
playing hard to get. He loved to be chased, and he

wanted me to fight for him. We'd been together a long time, and things had gotten stale."

"He asked for a divorce because he wanted you to prove your love?"

"Stranger things have happened in other people's relationships. And Donald was having a midlife crisis, which all men do. He even dyed his hair. I found a box of the stuff hidden in the back of a cabinet."

"Surely, if he'd wanted to make things work, he wouldn't have filed for divorce. That's a final statement."

She sank her teeth into a chunk of cookie crumble cake. "Who knows how Donald's mind worked? I thought I knew him, so it was a shock when I got the divorce papers. I suggested couple's counselling, talking therapies, maybe even a trial separation. I only suggested the last option because I was certain, when I was out of his life, he'd realize what he was missing out on and would crawl back."

"He didn't crawl?"

Brittany sniffed. "He would have."

"When Donald wasn't interested in doing anything to repair the relationship, you stalked him?"

"A wife has the right to know what her husband is doing, especially when he acts irrationally and hides things."

"Campbell mentioned you followed him and used cameras to watch him."

Brittany tutted and set to work on her second cake. "Campbell is a worse gossip than the biddies who come to my café and make a cup of tea last three hours. I thought the castle security detail were discreet, but that irritating agent is sharing my secrets." Her gaze traveled over me. "Why? What's so special about you?"

"Campbell just wants to scare me to confess I was your sidekick in Donald's murder."

She rolled her eyes. "He's tenacious. I'll give him that. But he's still wrong."

I wasn't sure what my next move should be, so I sipped tea and nibbled on the edge of a scone.

"Donald should have been grateful to me," Brittany said. "I tipped my whole life upside down to keep that man. I even moved."

"You moved?"

"So I could run that wretched café! When I learned Donald was packing his things and leaving our home, I found out where he was going."

"And you followed him?"

"Of course. I didn't want the saying, 'out of sight, out of mind,' to come true." She tossed her blonde hair over one shoulder. "I ran a Café Costel in Rose Acre Mount. It's about twenty miles from here. That's where we have our house."

"That's the cute village with all the thatched cottages?"

"It's a sleepy little place, but Donald's undertaking business took him all over the county, so it was no problem for him to move and not lose clients. As he was always saying, people die everywhere. But my job tied me to the café in that village. Donald was never generous with his money, so I couldn't stop working."

"What did you do?"

She beamed at me, looking so proud of herself. "I contacted the head office. I knew they were looking to expand, so I argued the case for opening a Café Costel in Audley St. Mary."

My stomach dropped, and I swallowed. "You only opened the café because Donald moved here?"

"It was so clever of me. It took me time to find out where he'd moved to, but I tracked him eventually and discovered he'd rented a place on the edge of this village. After sweet talking the letting company, I learned he'd taken a lease for two years, so he was intending to stay."

I felt sick. "So you put together a business proposal for opening a café right here? Opposite my café?"

"It was easy to convince the suits, given all the tourists that come to Audley Castle. I was certain it would be a smash, especially with me running it."

I stuffed the rest of the scone in my mouth and chewed furiously. I was losing my business because of this woman's unhealthy obsession with her husband. I grabbed another scone and ate it in two bites, mainly to prevent myself from yelling at Brittany.

"Slow down, Holly. You can't jog off that much cake."

I kept eating. How I wished I had a mean enough streak to change my statement. Then Brittany would be out of my life for good. Could I do it? Campbell would believe me in a second. He wanted to arrest Brittany for this murder. All I had to do was pretend I'd lied. I could say she intimidated me into giving her an alibi.

No. I couldn't do it. I thought I'd do anything to save my café, but I drew the line at sending an innocent woman to prison.

"I have an idea," Brittany said, oblivious to my contained rage. "Since Campbell believes we're working together, why don't we do just that?"

I swallowed my huge mouthful of scone. "Work together how?"

"Work to find the killer. It wasn't me, and you weren't my sidekick, so it must be somebody else. Possibly someone we know. I've most likely served them. What a thought. I've given coffee to a killer." She mock shivered.

I gritted my teeth. There was no way I'd work with Brittany. The woman was a menace. "We should leave the experts to do that."

Her bottom lip jutted out. "I haven't seen much expertise so far."

I couldn't disagree with that. "I'm interested in the man Donald argued with at the village green event. You were there when they fought. Do you know his name?"

"He's a nobody. Not important. Just a worn out old windbag, who should have retired a long time ago."

"He worked with Donald?"

"They did business together. Clifford Facey. He has a heart condition and barely leaves his house these days. He's in a supported living place." Brittany shuffled to the edge of her seat. "Since we're working together, I'll share my thoughts about the killer. Freddie Shah had a lot to gain from Donald's death." She waggled her eyebrows.

I bit my tongue. "I don't know Freddie Shah."

"He's a rival undertaker. And now Donald is dead, Freddie will make moves on the recently deceased. Audley St. Mary is prime pickings, given the average age of the residents is ninety-five on a good day. He'll be scooping up business and making a fortune."

Although I wasn't working with Brittany, I'd happily use the information she provided. "Where is Freddie based?"

"Bradwell Mallow. Two villages over. Donald and Freddie hated each other. They were always fighting for customers. Donald used to curse him out all the time. He even sabotaged a few of his burials."

"Do I want to know how?" Donald was a real piece of work for ruining such an important event in a family's life.

Brittany giggled. "Best you don't. But those two were sworn enemies."

"Have you told the police this information?"

"No, but only because every time they talk to me, I end up in tears and feel guilty for something I didn't do." She raised her eyebrows. "I can think clearly with you helping me. I know we can do this."

Nope. I still wasn't working with Brittany, no matter how hard she fake-liked me. "You should tell them about Freddie. If the rivalry was as serious as you claim, it gives him an excellent motive for murder."

Her eyes widened. "You're a natural at this sort of thing. We'd be great working together. I'm so glad we're friends."

I mumbled something that sounded like an agreement.

"I'll talk to the police tomorrow and point them toward Freddie. That'll take the heat off me, and I can get back to running my café."

And I'd get to work on finding Freddie and see what he knew about Donald's murder.

Brittany reached over and caught hold of my hand. "I know things have been difficult for you, with my café doing so well, and yours... not so much, but no hard feelings? It's just business, after all. And if things don't work out for you, I'm always looking to hire assistants. You'd be welcome to apply. No one ever wants to work the weekend shifts. And I know you have no social life."

I withdrew my hand. "How would you know that?"

She lifted one shoulder. "You're either working or walking your funny looking dog. And I've never seen you with a guy, so you're not married."

"I like to keep my personal life just that." How I kept my tone civil would remain one of life's unsolved mysteries.

"Whatever you think best. So, no hard feelings?"

"Sure." I just about managed not to upend the cakes on her head. This may just be business to Brittany, but my life was about to implode, thanks to her.

"Let's have more cake, and we can talk about something more interesting than murder." Brittany topped up her mug.

"I should get going. Busy day tomorrow."

"You are funny, Holly. Your café is never busy. Have more coffee."

"No, I'll leave you to it."

"If you're sure. Leave the cakes, though."

I unclenched my hands. As I was realizing, business rivalry was an excellent motive for murder. "Bring back the hamper when you're done."

"Of course. And thanks for the chat, Holly. You're a real gal pal."

As I hurried out, quickly kicking the high heel Meatball had chewed under the shoe rack, my thoughts turned to my mortality.

It was time I visited a local undertaker and planned my funeral. And maybe Brittany's, too.

Chapter 9

"Thanks for fitting me in at such short notice." I was settled in a comfortable high-backed armchair in a pleasant office in Shah and Sons' Undertakers. Meatball was tucked by my feet.

When I'd called to make my appointment, they'd been able to fit me in at lunchtime the next day, so I'd made the sacrifice of shutting the café and headed to Bradwell Mallow to speak to Freddie Shah about a funeral plan. And maybe a murder.

"I'm always happy to make time for a new customer." Freddie sat opposite me, dressed in a dark suit. He was around sixty, skinny, and pale. A few weeks working outside would bring color to his cheeks, but he fit the stereotypical role of an undertaker wonderfully, with his sad eyes and calm manner.

"I like to have a plan for everything," I said.

"That's good to hear. Although, I must admit I'm surprised someone with so few ties is thinking about death. Most people don't think about the end until they own property and have dependents. From the information you gave me, I see you have neither."

"I have Meatball. He's my fur baby."

His expression turned sympathetic. "We have excellent prepaid funeral plans to suit all requirements."

I lowered my gaze and attempted to look sad. "There's been a recent death in Audley St. Mary, and it made me think about my demise. I decided I shouldn't put this off. You never know what's around the corner."

"Oh, of course. I heard about the... events in Audley St. Mary." He checked through the information I'd emailed him.

"It was shocking. Everyone in the village is talking about it." I lifted my gaze. "You must have known Donald."

Freddie paused for a second. "I did."

"I'm sorry for your loss. Were you close?"

"No, not close." He opened a glossy brochure. "Perhaps you'd like to look at our range of coffins. I have something for all budgets."

"Of course. And I mean no offense by this, but I'd have gone to Donald to plan my funeral, given he was local to Audley St. Mary. I wonder what'll happen to his business now he's gone."

"I couldn't say. I find my younger clients prefer sustainable options. We provide wicker or cardboard."

My eyebrows rose. "Wouldn't a cardboard coffin break?"

"Oh, no. They can handle a fully grown adult with ease. We interweave the cardboard for strength and use industrial sealants. Only the best here."

"That's good to know. Did Donald provide cardboard coffins?"

"I had little to do with his business. Let's set aside the coffin for a moment. Do you want to be buried or cremated?"

I shuddered. I'd given no thought to what would happen to me when I died, but I should. I didn't want to leave a mess behind and have people grieving for me and not knowing what my last wishes were. "Err... I know burial plots are scarce. Did you know that was where Donald's body was found? In an open grave."

His eyes narrowed a fraction. "I heard. Most unfortunate."

"The police believe it wasn't an accident. I actually saw his body." I made a show of dabbing my eyes with a tissue. "At first, I thought he'd simply fallen into the grave."

"Well, there are hazards in our line of work."

"The police have been questioning so many people. Have they been to see you?"

Freddie eased back in his seat. "I had a brief conversation with an individual. I wasn't able to tell him anything useful. I didn't mix in the same circles as Donald." He opened a different page of the brochure. "What kind of service would you like? Do you follow a particular religion?"

"Um... Not really. I want something simple. Could I have a favorite pop song played? Would that be appropriate? Or is it only hymns? I have a few from my school days I like."

"Depending on where you hold the service, you can have any music you like. I once conducted a service for the lead singer in a death metal band. I forget the exact name of the tune they brought in him to, but it was something like "Slaughter Them All and Drink Their Blood." I may have gotten that around the wrong way. The mourners enjoyed it. Several of them were... I believe it's called head banging."

"No death metal for me. I'm more of an eighties pop music girl."

"Whatever you wish. Here's a list of questions you'll find useful to consider when planning your service." Freddie pushed a sheet of paper toward me. "It's difficult to consider your own death, but many find it a comfort once they've gone through the process."

"I'm realizing that." I looked through the questions. This visit had gotten me thinking about more than Donald's murder, but I had to focus on one thing at a time. "What kind of service will Donald be having?"

"I couldn't tell you."

"Are you organizing it? It would help me to see what someone else has planned."

"I'm not."

"Will you go to his funeral? You must have done plenty of business together over the years."

Freddie's nostrils flared. "We never worked together. I doubt I'll attend the service. And I suspect there'll be few people mourning his loss."

I feigned surprise. "Donald wasn't popular?"

"Not from my experience." He leaned forward, a dash of color streaking up his neck. "I suspect he arranged the cheapest send-off for himself. He'll show his miserly colors to the end."

I set down the questions I'd been scanning. "I did some business with Donald. I was alarmed how he ran things."

A slight smirk flickered across Freddie's face. "Let me guess, he argued over an invoice? What line of work are you in?"

"Catering. I run a café in Audley St. Mary and recently expanded into providing food for wakes. Donald would recommend me and receive a percentage of the profits. But when I submitted my last invoice, he asked me to reduce it. It had me worried. I keep costs as low as possible for wakes. The grieving family and friends have so many other things to pay for."

"That's decent of you. Unfortunately, that thought would never have entered Donald's head. All he was interested in was making more money. I suspect if you'd cut costs and passed the savings on through him, he'd have charged the original amount to the mourners and pocketed the difference."

"That's theft!"

"Only if he got caught. And Donald was excellent at playing the benevolent middleman and saying he was doing it for the family of the deceased. It was an act." Freddie pressed his lips together. "Although I wouldn't ever wish anyone dead, you had a lucky escape from taking on more work he directed your way."

"Donald didn't escape, though." I lowered my gaze again. "I can't stop thinking about who killed him. It's unsettled everyone in Audley St. Mary."

"They'll come around when they learn what a miser he was. Everyone in our business called him Sinister Scrooge behind his back." Freddie chuckled to himself as he rubbed his hands together. "It's a pity. The man had the potential to be brilliant. When he started, he had an excellent partner to guide him. A real gentleman, who provided the old school flourishes to services you don't see anymore."

He must mean Clifford Facey, but I couldn't let on I knew. "Who was that?"

"It was a long time ago. Working with Donald made him ill, and when Clifford developed a heart condition, he sold up. He eventually moved to the retirement complex on the edge of Audley St. Mary."

"Silver Vale?"

"Yes. I get good custom from there."

I resisted the urge to wrinkle my nose. This was the man Brittany had mentioned, and the same man who'd come into my café just before Donald's body was discovered. She'd dismissed him as a suspect, but I wasn't so quick to do the same. "Did Clifford go on to set up his own business?"

"I encouraged him to, but the fight had left him. Dealing with Donald, and with his health declining, Clifford was exhausted. He turned to drink." A wistful look entered Freddie's eyes. "When they first started the business, they were so excited. We used to be friends and would catch up over a drink. They always said they'd look out for each other. But after the deceit... I've said too much."

"What deceit?"

"My apologies. This meeting isn't about my good old days or, rather, my bad old days." Freddie stood from his seat. "Let me show you the coffin models to help you decide."

"I get to look at the coffins?" My mind was whirling with questions. Donald had made Clifford sick and deceived him. They were excellent motives for murder. And from the way Freddie talked, he also had a reason for wanting Donald dead.

"I have a room dedicated to my coffins. It's along the hallway." Freddie leaned across the desk and patted my hand. "No need to be alarmed. I assure you, they're empty."

I gulped. I hadn't even considered that ghoulish option.

Meatball whined and hid his nose under a paw.

Freddie lifted his hands. "Forgive my undertaker's humor. Sometimes, being around such a tragic, occasionally dark business means we need to lift the mood with a joke."

"I imagine you must. Especially when you have to arrange the funeral of a murder victim."

"Indeed. Shall we?" He gestured to the door.

I didn't want to look at coffins, but I still had questions. Had Freddie grown sick of Donald's deceitful business practices and taken matters into his own hands to erase a problem? Or was Clifford recovered enough from his heart condition and had returned for revenge?

Freddie winced and rubbed his shoulder. "Excuse me. Old age gets us all." He opened the office door and gestured for me to go through first. "Turn right, and its two doors along on the left-hand side. May I ask your budget for your final party?"

"Oh! Running my own business doesn't leave much money at the end of the month. Nothing too extravagant. No ivory or mahogany coffins for me."

"Which is why our pre-paid plans are a wonderful option. You pay them off in instalments. Put down a deposit and then pay over one year, two years, even up to five years. I'll make sure I can accommodate you. We won't leave you coffinless when the time comes."

"Um... thanks."

Freddie led me to a closed door and turned to face me. "Rest assured, we're not all like Donald. My family has been undertakers going back five generations. We understand the needs and issues that arise when a death occurs. Many of them are due to lack of planning. We don't want to give anyone a pauper's grave unless we have to."

I nodded, suddenly nervous about entering a room full of coffins.

"Now, allow me to show you your final place of rest."

I sucked in a deep breath and squinted as the door opened. I wasn't sure what I'd been expecting, but the room was pleasant. It was warmly lit, and there was a lemon scent in the air. There were also fresh vases of flowers dotted around. The coffin lids were open, so there'd be no surprises leaping out and scaring me.

"Take your time and look around. Let me know if there's anything that takes your eye. The luxury range is to the right, and a more affordable range, including the wicker and the cardboard coffins, are on the left." Freddie's gaze went to Meatball. "I also have contacts at the pet cemetery, for when the time comes."

Meatball bared his teeth at Freddie.

I shoved that awful thought away. Meatball would live for as long as I did. "Who'd have thought making a funeral plan was so complicated?"

"It doesn't need to be. Ask any questions you have to make things simple."

I wandered along the rows of coffins with Meatball. "I'm not sure if I'll have my funeral in a church. St. Mary's is beautiful, but I don't attend services."

"I didn't think I recognized you from any local services." Freddie remained a respectful distance away. "I often visit that church. I was even at the memorial service held on the day Donald was discovered."

I turned and stared at him. Freddie had just put himself at the crime scene. "I didn't know that."

"The vicar gives an excellent service. Even if you're not of a particular faith, it may be worth you attending. His lessons are valuable to all."

"I'll think about it. I like Reverend Liskard."

"He's a sensible man and always helping those in need. If you're considering that church for your final resting place, the burial plots aren't cheap, though. And I believe they're reserved for those who were born in Audley St. Mary. But they have a wonderful wildflower meadow where ashes can be scattered if you go that route."

I resisted the urge to shudder again. "Does Donald have a plot at St. Mary's church?" I studied a brown, angular wicker coffin with brass handles.

He paused. "You have a considerable interest in Donald's death. May I ask why?"

I kept my attention on the coffin. "His murder happened in the place I live, and I saw his body."

"You mentioned that."

"And... I'm somewhat involved in the investigation, since the police's main suspect asked me to provide her with an alibi. It was a legitimate alibi, of course, but it made me curious about Donald's life and death."

"Well, that is quite an involvement." Freddie cleared his throat. "All I will say about the man is he was driven by how much money he had. There was a time when he was undercutting every undertaker in the area. We approached him as a group and suggested he stopped."

"What did you do to make him stop?"

"We cautioned him against driving down prices for the sake of getting more business. When that happens, it becomes a race to the bottom, and people end up running businesses that aren't profitable. They're forced to do things they don't enjoy to make ends meet."

Those words brought me back to Campbell's comments about providing budget cakes. It just felt wrong.

Freddie adjusted his tie. "I didn't approve of Donald's business model, but I respected him as a person. His death was a tragedy, but none of the undertakers within a fifty-mile radius will be mourning. Donald left a large hole in the community, and we'll be stepping forward to fill it. He'd have done nothing less."

I glanced at Freddie out of the corner of my eye. He despised Donald. He had a clear motive for wanting him out of the way, and he'd revealed he'd been at the church when Donald was killed. All the alarm bells were ringing that he was a prime suspect.

"Any decisions made?" Freddie said after a few minutes of silence.

"I'm not certain. I need to think about it some more. I haven't even thought about flowers or where I want my service held. It's so overwhelming."

"Put down a deposit today for a pre-paid plan, and you can come back anytime you like to tweak the finer details."

"A deposit? Oh, I... I couldn't do that." I clutched my purse. I couldn't afford a deposit on a new pair of shoes, let alone an expensive funeral plan.

"A ten percent deposit will guarantee your place. We can work out the rest later. You can take an information pack, talk to friends and family to see if they have suggestions, and then come back. And you can call me if you have any questions."

"I'll talk to friends first and then set up the plan."

Freddie walked over and caught hold of my elbow, propelling me to the door and along the hallway. "Most people never get the courage to discuss their final plans. You're a brave woman, Holly. Don't let that courage fail you at the last hurdle." He stopped by the desk, opened a drawer, and pulled out a card reader. "I'll put you on our basic plan, and when your café takes off, you can upgrade to all the ivory and mahogany a successful business woman desires."

I looked at the door he blocked. I wasn't getting out. "That sounds fine." I rifled through my purse and flipped it open. I didn't have enough money in my current account or my business account, but I could use my credit card. It was for emergencies only. I eased it out and hovered it in the air.

Freddie pressed the card reader against my credit card. It beeped, and he took it away. "That's strange. Your card was rejected."

I checked the date, it was still valid.

"Let's try again. I'll cancel the transaction, so you don't get charged twice. We only need one coffin for your final farewell." Freddie pressed a few more buttons then held the reader out to me.

My hand trembled as I pressed the card against it. It gave another beep.

His forehead furrowed. "I'm sorry. Your card has been declined. Do you have another we could use?"

I stuffed my card into my purse. "No. Only that one."

"You should get onto your bank. You have a problem to deal with." Freddie's gaze ran over me as he placed the card reader back into the drawer and snapped it shut.

"Thanks. I will. And I appreciate your time." I hurried past him and out the door, Meatball trotting along beside me as my cheeks flamed.

My finances were in worse shape than I'd realized, but I'd deal with the bank later. Although flooded with embarrassment and feeling more than a little guilty about lying to Freddie, I'd obtained valuable information.

I had two new murder suspects.

Chapter 10

I made up for closing at lunchtime by staying open two hours later that evening. I'd gotten extra customers through the door, but I was exhausted. My feet hurt, and my eyes were gritty. I couldn't do these long days forever, or I'd end up needing that wicker coffin sooner than I thought.

After I'd said farewell to the last customer and locked the door, I pulled out my bank cards. A quick check of my online banking revealed I'd used my credit card three times that month. I was certain those transactions had gone through in the previous month, but I'd had to cover essential bills. I couldn't bake if I didn't have power.

It was no wonder they refused my down payment on a funeral plan. I was almost at my credit limit, and it was only halfway through the month. I should become as cutthroat as Donald and figure out how to make more money out of people.

I looked around my pretty café and shook my head. That wasn't me.

The cakes were covered, any leftovers that couldn't be salvaged had been recycled, and I was leaning against the counter, planning tomorrow's menu, when someone thudded on the café door.

I looked up to see a short, stocky woman with close-cropped dark hair. She wore black jeans and a bomber jacket. "Sorry, I'm closed for the evening. I open at seven tomorrow morning."

"I'm not here to eat." She held up a sheet of paper.
I walked over and looked at it. My stomach
dropped to my feet and bounced up again, almost
making me choke. "You're a bailiff!"

"I'm here to collect an unpaid debt. Are you Holly
Holmes?" The woman's dark eyes were lasered on me.

"Yes, I'm Holly. But I've paid all my bills. I have a
few outstanding for this month, but I'll get around to
them. I'm not that late paying for anything."

"Read this. You've missed three payments on the
catering equipment you bought on credit."

I'd been so panicked by her arrival, I'd only
skimmed the paperwork. I took a steadying breath
and read through it carefully. It was my contract from
KACE Supplies.

"There's been a mistake. I've missed one payment,
and I called to let them know I'd make it up as soon
as I could."

"You've missed more than one. You've been sent
several letters asking for payment and the interest on
top."

I glanced over my shoulder at the pile of bills. I
hadn't been opening them since I knew bad news
would be inside. "I must have missed the letters.
Maybe they were sent to the wrong address."

"I'm not here to cause trouble, Miss Holmes, but
you must repay the debt. Have you got the funds
available? I can take payment from any card."

I considered my credit card. "How much do you
need?"

"Fifteen hundred. And the interest."

My mouth went bone dry, and I grew lightheaded.
"I don't have that kind of money. As you can see, this
is a small place. Why so much?"

She lifted one shoulder. "The interest rate on the
debts with this company is sky high. You should have
kept up with the payments."

"I'll call them first thing tomorrow. I'll figure something out. This is a misunderstanding."

"They want payment now, which is why they sent me. And I'm not going anywhere until I get what you owe."

"Give me a minute." I pressed my hand against my sweaty forehead, certain I was about to faint. I'd never gotten myself into such bad debt before.

There was a scrabbling of claws on the tiled floor as Meatball dashed into the café. He jumped up my leg and whined as he licked my hand.

"You shouldn't be in here." I was so glad to have my little dog by my side. He always knew when I was distressed.

"Miss Holmes, make this easy on both of us. If you can't service your debt, let me in. I'll take the equipment back, and the debt will be repaid."

I sucked in several deep breaths. "If you take my equipment, I can't bake. I run a café. What am I supposed to sell?"

"I'm sorry, but that's not my problem. You should have paid your bills when they were due."

I was tempted to run out the back and ignore her, but several villagers had stopped outside and were watching the show. The news of my debt would be all over Audley St. Mary by the morning if I didn't deal with this.

I slid the bolts and turned the key before pulling open the door. "Come in."

She wiped her feet on the mat. "Thanks. Let's not make this unpleasant. I'll do a valuation on the equipment, which will include a depreciation because of use, and only take what I have to."

"You can't take anything. I need it all. I'll have to close if I lose any equipment."

Her gaze shifted around the café. "Then pay your bills. I'll take the money, and you'll never see me again. Unless, of course, you get in debt again."

Meatball growled, and his hackles rose.

The bailiff glared down at him. "Control your dog. I've dealt with the little ones before, and they're vicious."

"Meatball would never hurt you. He can sense I'm worried and is protecting me."

"Get rid of him, or I will." The bailiff took a step toward Meatball.

"Is there a problem?"

My gaze snapped up. Campbell stood in the doorway, his sunglasses in one hand. I hadn't even heard him open the door.

"No problem. We're just doing some business." The bailiff still glared at Meatball, who stood in front of me.

Campbell looked at me. "Holly, do you need a hand?"

"I'm... I'm not sure. This woman is a bailiff. I've gotten into debt, and she's here to collect." It felt lousy to reveal my situation, but keeping it concealed had only made things worse.

The bailiff turned to Campbell. "It's legit. I've got the paperwork here."

"Let me see." Campbell marched over and snatched the paperwork off her. He read through it then glanced at me. "You really are in trouble."

My cheeks flamed hot. "I'm handling it."

"Badly." His stony gaze shifted, spearing into the bailiff. "You're not a bailiff. You're a debt collector. And you can't take items from inside this business. You know the rules."

She squared her shoulders. "This client isn't servicing her debts."

"You still can't take her equipment."

"Is that true?" I whispered.

Campbell passed the paperwork back to her. "And the address is wrong."

"It isn't! It doesn't leave the office unless it's been verified."

I wasn't certain what was going on, but Campbell was sticking up for me.

"The paperwork is incomplete, so you can't collect on the debt. You're here without a valid reason."

She scanned the paperwork and sighed. "It took me an hour to drive here, and all for nothing."

"Does that mean I don't have to repay the debt?" Hope flickered inside me like the fragile candle flame on a pink iced birthday cake.

"You'll have to repay," Campbell said, "but this lot needs to get their paperwork in order before you do. And next time, send a real bailiff, not a hired thug."

The bailiff, who apparently wasn't a bailiff, stuffed the paperwork inside her jacket. She stomped out, climbed into a white van, and screeched away.

It was only when she'd gone that I saw the black SUV on the other side of the road. The back window was cracked down, and someone peeked out.

"Holly, take a seat. You look like you're about to faint." Campbell guided me to a chair and eased me into it, Meatball glued to my side.

I gulped in air, still reeling from the shock of almost losing my business. "I hate to be a damsel in distress, but you saved me. Thank you."

"Don't thank me. Thank the Audley family."

"They knew about the bailiff's visit?" I looked at the black SUV.

"I'm sure they didn't, but we were driving past, and my passenger saw you arguing with the debt collector. They insisted I stop and assist you."

"Who is it? Lady Philippa?"

"I can't say."

"You won't say. May I thank her personally?"

"Stay in your seat until you get color back in your cheeks." Campbell crouched in front of me. "The Audley family look after their own."

"They consider me a part of the family?"

"According to... whoever I have in the back of my vehicle, you're an important part of Audley St. Mary. That's what matters." A small smirk crossed Campbell's face. "And of course, they like your cakes. So do I. We don't want you going anywhere."

Learning such an influential family considered me important had me almost as flustered as nearly losing the contents of my kitchen because of an unpaid debt. "I'm fortunate you were passing. Let me make you a coffee. And you must take cake as a thank you. For your mystery passenger, too."

"No need. And it's not fortunate. I deliberately drove past to see if you were open. I planned on dropping off my passenger and then talking to you."

"About what?"

Campbell stood, the faint hint of kindness gone as quickly as it had arrived. He slid his sunglasses into place. "Despite me telling you not to, you're still snooping into Donald's murder."

I leaned down and petted Meatball. "I am?"

"You visited Freddie Shah and questioned him."

"How do you... never mind." Campbell knew my every move. "If you must know, I went to talk to him about a funeral plan."

"You're planning on dying soon, are you?"

"You should be so lucky."

He crossed his arms over his chest. "My life would be simpler with you out of the way."

I glared at him. Campbell's sunglasses hid his eyes, but he most likely glared back. I wasn't backing down, and I wasn't stopping asking questions. Campbell could intimidate all he liked, but I'd get to the truth.

Meatball's soft whine broke the tension, and I reached down and petted his head again.

"Holly, this isn't something to keep you entertainment. Donald was killed."

"That's why I'm investigating. I'm not doing it for fun!"

"I mean, his killer is still on the loose, and you poking around could draw whoever did it to you. If you get close to the truth, they'll silence you."

I shivered and clutched my hands around my waist. I hadn't considered that.

Campbell sat in the chair opposite me. "Give me full disclosure about what you've learned so far."

"Why?"

"Because if you don't, I'll call back that bailiff and help her take your kitchen equipment. That would give you something else to worry about, and you'd leave this investigation alone."

I massaged my forehead with my fingers. He probably would do that. "I'll tell you what I know, if you do the same."

"I'm listening."

That wasn't the response I wanted, but it was the best I'd get. "I haven't just been to see Freddie. I also visited Brittany. And I learned interesting information from both of them."

"Go on."

"Brittany still loved Donald. Maybe that love was obsessional, but she was convinced they'd get back together. Why kill him if that was her plan?"

"Keep talking."

I pursed my lips. "Freddie has a better motive than Brittany. He also had the opportunity. He was at the memorial service at St. Mary's church on the day Donald was murdered."

"What was his motive?"

"To get Donald's business. They hated each other, and Freddie said he was part of a group of undertakers who ganged up on Donald and warned him to stop playing dirty. He pretended he respected Donald, but I suspect he's been dancing around his office since Donald was killed."

"It wasn't Freddie."

"How can you be so certain?"

"Because I've spoken to him. Did you notice the way he held his right arm?"

"He seemed stiff. Freddie said it was an age thing. I get it. Even I groan when I've been sitting for too long, and I'm younger than Freddie."

"You should stretch after your workouts. But it's not that. Freddie recently had shoulder surgery. He wouldn't have been able to lift that headstone."

My mouth twisted to the side. "I didn't know that."

"What a surprise, since you're not trained in the art of detecting and solving murders. I'm still looking at Brittany."

"I may not be trained in super sleuthing, but you're wrong to look at her. Donald was mean, but Brittany loved him. And don't forget, she didn't have time to kill him because she was bothering me, using my bathroom, and eating my cake."

"You only have half the story about Brittany."

"Tell me what I'm missing. Convince me she did it." I sat back and waited.

Campbell shrugged. "Brittany was leaving threatening notes on Donald's car. She made it clear he'd be sorry for what he'd done. She even damaged a hearse by scratching the paintwork. The woman is unhinged. Obsession causes irrational behavior, and love quickly turns to hatred. Donald turned Brittany down one too many times, and when she finally figured out he was done with her, she snapped."

"That's all new information to me, but none of it is relevant. Brittany still didn't have time to commit the murder."

"If you'd been to super sleuth school, you'd know no murder timeline is perfect. People get the time wrong or misremember because of stress."

"Not me."

"Even you, Holly Holmes. You're not perfect. Demonstrated by your terrible tack of financial planning."

I snitched my nose. Nobody liked to have their flaws pointed out. "Brittany and Freddie mentioned a former business partner of Donald's, called Clifford Facey. Have you spoken to him?"

"I've spoken to everyone of relevance. Or are you suggesting I don't know how to do my job?"

Hmmm, the prickly version of Campbell was back in the room. "I'm suggesting you're unhealthily obsessed with charging Brittany for a murder she didn't do. There are other suspects."

"And they've all been followed up and dismissed."

I shook my head. Campbell was the most irritating man I'd ever met. "Then I have nothing more to tell you. Now you. Share the rest."

He stayed silent.

"I've got leftover cookie crumble cake in the back. Would that convince you to talk?"

A smile flickered across his face. "I'll tell you two things so you can rest easy we're not incompetent."

"I look forward to that."

A muscle twitched in his jaw. "Tread carefully, Holly. I'm being polite because the Audley family likes you."

"You do, too."

"It's up for debate." Campbell drew in a breath. "Donald had a scrap of torn cloth in his hand. We believe he reached for his attacker and caught hold of their clothing before he fell."

"Was it from a coat, a dress, or something else?"

"We're looking into that. Brittany's closet is being examined."

I groaned. "Not Brittany again. Unless it's leopard print or bright pink, it won't belong to her."

"Second clue. Pay attention. There were marks on Donald's clothing."

"What kind of marks?"

Campbell wagged a finger in the air. "That's all you're getting."

"Oil? Paint? Dirt? Give me something."

"None of the above."

I considered the clues. "This torn cloth and the stains are leading you to Brittany?"

"That's all you're getting. Where's my cake?"

I huffed out a breath. "You don't deserve it. You only gave me half the information. Now, I have more questions to puzzle through."

"You're fortunate I gave you any information."

I stood from the table to get his cake. A deal was a deal. I paused and turned back to Campbell. "I've got an idea. I want to prove to you that you're wrong."

"I'm never wrong."

Arrogant man. "The killer was Freddie or Donald's former business partner, Clifford. So, how about this: Let's investigate them together."

Chapter 11

"I've never been spoken to so rudely!" I paced in front of Meatball in the café kitchen the next morning. Rage had bubbled through me all night as I'd replayed my final words with Mr. Idiot Security Agent. "All I'd suggested was we worked together, but Campbell was too arrogant to think anyone else can solve this mystery. Everyone needs help."

Meatball raised a paw and whined.

"I know! I'm a smart, put together businesswoman. I can do anything I set my mind to." My gaze flicked to the pile of bills. Well, almost anything. I grabbed a croissant from the chiller and sank my teeth into it. I'd been stress eating since yesterday evening, after Campbell's rude dismissal of my offer.

I pulled out Meatball's dried food and gave him a healthy portion. He dived in.

I ate my croissant and kept walking around the kitchen. "He said I was worse than the little old ladies in the village and needed something to occupy my spare time. As if I have any of that."

Meatball was too busy filling his furry face, but he lowered his tail, suggesting he understood how I felt.

"We'll show him. I'm solving this murder, and we'll make Campbell look like a puffed up fool." I grabbed a small wicker basket and opened the chiller again. "It's likely I've already talked to the killer, but if not, there's someone else we need to see. A final puzzle piece."

Meatball cocked his head.

"And you're the perfect companion to help." I shut the chiller and placed the basket down. "A quick shower. I'll pick my best treats, and then we're going to Silver Vale retirement village."

Meatball put his paw over his nose.

"The oldies will love you. You can pose as a therapy pet. Just be on your best behavior, and no stealing the old ladies' cookies."

He wagged his tail and looked as innocent as a puppy, but Meatball was almost as bad as me with sweet treats.

Half an hour later, and after putting a sign up to let customers know I'd be late opening, I was excited by the prospect of finding Donald's killer and besting Campbell.

I walked the twenty minutes to Silver Vale, giving me time to think through how I'd approach Clifford Facey. I decided on the direct route.

As I grew near the single-story building with pretty flower beds and painted benches outside, I discovered a small group of residents doing yoga. Some of their downward facing dogs were impressive.

Meatball forgot his promise to behave and raced over to the group. He ran around them, sniffing faces and causing a few participants to lose their balance and tumble over.

An elderly gent in a red sweat suit caught hold of Meatball and petted him.

I dashed over. "I'm sorry. Meatball gets excited when people roll around on the ground. He thinks they're playing and wants to join in."

The man continued to scratch Meatball in the sweet spot at the base of his tail. "No harm done. He reminds me of my old dog. What a handsome boy you have."

"I think so, but I'm biased, since we belong to each other."

The man smiled up at me. "I've not seen you here before. Are you visiting someone?"

"Yes. Clifford Facey." I glanced around the group, hoping he'd be present.

"You won't find him doing yoga. There's only one activity Clifford enjoys." The man mimed lifting a large glass to his lips and downing it, making a glug, glug, glug noise in the back of his throat.

"Could you tell me where he lives? I brought him breakfast treats. It's a surprise." I opened the basket for him to have a peek.

The man's eyes widened. "I'll give you the information you need in exchange for one blueberry muffin."

"Deal!" I handed over the muffin and collected Meatball, who was attempting an over enthusiastic lick of the man's face while sniffing the muffin at the same time.

"Head along the right-hand path. Clifford lives in the third building on the left. Number twenty. You may need to knock for a few minutes. He's not an early riser."

After thanking him, I hurried away with Meatball, located Clifford's home, and knocked.

Clifford looked as bedraggled as the first time we met, but this time, he wore a checked green robe over plaid pajamas. He had bags under his eyes, and gray stubble dusted his chin. "Huh! Who are you? I thought you were the warden coming to complain again."

"I'm not here to complain. Are you Clifford Facey?"

He scratched his fingers through his stubble. "I was the last time I checked. What can I do for you, young lady?"

"It's the other way around. I'm Holly Holmes, and I run the café in Audley St. Mary. You stopped by the other day."

"Oh, sure. I thought you looked familiar. Why do you need my help? I'm no baker." He chuckled. "I make a mean home brew, though."

I drew in a breath. "I have questions about Donald Barclay. You used to work with him?"

His bleary eyes snapped into focus, and his gaze traveled over me slowly. Not in a creepy way, but as if he was assessing me for threats.

"You worked for Donald, too?" he finally said.

"Indirectly. And I'm not here to cause trouble, but I would like to talk. I assume you know what happened to him?"

"Sure do. Everybody does." Clifford's gaze went to Meatball, and his expression softened. "Who's this wonderful chap?"

"His name's Meatball."

Meatball raised his paw to be shaken, and Clifford bent and solemnly shook hand to paw. "I've been thinking about getting a dog. It gets lonely here. Rita's been dead three years, and I get bored staring at the TV. And my daughter is worthless. She only visits when she wants money."

"I can recommend a dog. Meatball is an excellent companion."

"I trust anyone who likes animals." Clifford straightened slowly and rubbed the base of his spine. "I'll tell you what I know about Donald, but it isn't pretty."

"I'm prepared for that. And thank you. I've brought breakfast. Are you hungry?"

His eyes lit up. "You should have said. My cupboards are bare." He stepped back and gestured us inside.

Clifford's home was compact but tidy. There was a single chair set in front of a large screen TV in the living room and a small table in one corner with two foldout chairs set against it. Other than a cabinet with a few curiosities in it, the place looked like he'd only just moved in.

"We'll sit in the garden. It's my favorite place. I enjoy watching the wildlife."

"Sounds perfect."

"I'll make coffee."

"I can do that if you'd like me to."

He chuckled again. "I may look like a worn out old fool, but I can fend for myself. You get set up outside, and I'll be out in a few minutes."

I headed through a set of double doors with Meatball. It was clear this was where Clifford spent his money. The garden was alive with color. Not only were there bird feeding stations but also numerous insect houses, bird boxes, and a cute little mound with a sign over the top saying hedgehog home.

Meatball got busy sniffing, while I arranged the croissants and muffins on a large napkin.

Clifford came out with a tray with our coffee. He'd also brought plates and knives and a pot of strawberry preserves.

"You have a beautiful garden," I said.

"I like it. It keeps me occupied."

Meatball bounded over for another pet.

"He must have smelled the treats." Clifford grinned as he set down the tray. "A few of the other old codgers have dogs, so I always slip them biscuits."

I arranged the table while Clifford spoiled Meatball.

Clifford settled in a seat, and I sat opposite him. He pulled a silver flask from his robe pocket and poured a generous helping into his coffee and then offered it to me.

I lifted a hand. "I'm not one for the hard stuff, whatever the time of day."

"You'd have turned to drink if you'd spent too much time with Donald. Cheers." He lifted his mug and took a long drink before setting it down and smacking his lips together. "What do you want to know about Devious Donald?"

"The police believe he was murdered."

"Couldn't have happened to a nicer guy."

I stared at him with wide eyes.

"I make no apologies for that comment. The man was a cheat and a tyrant, and anyone who asks for my opinion of Donald will get the same answer."

"What did he do to you?"

Clifford let out a long sigh. "We were supposed to be equal partners. We set up business together after years of friendship." He drank more laced coffee and took a croissant. "I've never had a head for figures, so Donald said he'd deal with that side of things. He showed me the accounts regularly, and I never thought to question what he did with the money."

"What was he doing with it?"

"Skimming off the top and putting it into an account that was hard to trace."

"That money should have been shared equally between you?"

"Exactly. Equal partners in everything. I questioned him a couple of times about withdrawals on the statements, but he said it was an expansion savings fund, so I didn't think it was strange." Clifford kept drinking his coffee and adding more alcohol. "I was an idiot. People even warned me about Donald, but I wouldn't hear a bad word against him. He was my friend, so he'd never cheat me."

"How did you figure out what was going on?" I was so engrossed in the conversation, I hadn't eaten a thing.

"I overheard Donald arguing with Brittany. She'd found statements from his secret account and confronted him. She thought he was leaving her for another woman and that money would fund his new life."

"What did he tell her?"

"He denied everything but said it was his private savings and he'd use it to buy them a villa abroad. He'd always told me the money was for both of us to secure our future." Clifford looked over his garden, his eyes hazed with tears. "I didn't know what to do. I loved working as an undertaker. It may sound strange, given we deal with the dead, but I helped those left behind and made sure the deceased got a good sendoff. I got satisfaction from that. I thought that's why Donald did it, too. But he just saw an opportunity to exploit vulnerable people. I include myself in that. He used my blind trust to exploit me."

Before I could ask more questions, there was a knock at the front door, and a key turned in the lock. "Hey-hoo! Warden calling."

Clifford shoved the flask into his robe pocket and pressed a finger to his lips. "I'm not supposed to drink. I've already had one warning from Old Frosty Drawers. The warden is a stickler for the rules."

A few seconds later, a skinny, gray-haired woman poked her head out the back door. "It's nice to see you up so early, Clifford. And you have company. How lovely."

"This is my new friend, Holly. She dropped by so we could have breakfast together." Clifford discreetly winked at me.

The warden regarded me with ample suspicion. "You run the village café, don't you?"

I nodded. "And you always buy an almond croissant and an oat milk latte at the weekend."

"Well remembered. I do. I hope Clifford is behaving."

"I always behave." He raised his mug at her.

"I had complaints last night. You were up late and playing music loudly. Our residents are early birds and need their sleep. And one lady said you were drunk again. We've talked about this."

"Everyone is welcome to join me for a night cap. The old biddies might have a good time with a few drinks inside them."

The warden arched a gray eyebrow. "Enjoy your breakfast. And don't forget your doctor's appointment at noon."

Clifford rolled his eyes as she turned and left. "She's such a busybody. Always poking about in my business."

"I'm sure she only does it because she cares," I said.

"She does it because she gets paid to. Nosy old bag." He topped up his coffee from the flask.

"I'm no medical expert, but if you're not well, you shouldn't be drinking so early or so much."

He waved away my comment. "There's nothing they can do for me. They give me medication to keep me alive, but it's my heart. The doctor reckons it was damaged from the stress of being cheated by Donald."

"I'm sorry to hear that. Do you mind me asking how much he stole from you?"

"Too much, and I haven't gotten any of it back. I don't know how he managed it, but that money went missing. Maybe he spent it, or it's in a secret trust fund no one will ever find. Serves him right he was killed. The greedy man shouldn't have taken it. I'm certain I wasn't the only one he conned."

"You're probably right. I've also spoken to another undertaker, Freddie Shah."

"Him! He's almost as bad as Donald. Comes over caring and considerate, but he's always rubbing his hands together when money is concerned."

I thought about his tactics to get me to sign up for a funeral plan and nodded. "Freddie said he still respected Donald, despite their rivalry."

"What a load of tosh! Let me show you his version of respect." Clifford pulled himself out of the chair and staggered inside. He returned with a file. "That's respect for you. Freddie paid for these ads to be in the local paper."

I opened the file and rifled through half a dozen clippings. They declared Donald's undertaker service cheated people and he couldn't be trusted with the fragile needs of the deceased.

Clifford slumped into his seat and pulled out his flask again. "They loathed each other. When I heard Donald had been shoved into a grave and crushed, my thoughts went to Freddie. He'd see it as poetic justice, Donald going out that way."

"I wondered about that. But I don't think Freddie is fit enough to commit the crime. He's recently had shoulder surgery."

He scrubbed at his chin again. "That's a pity. I don't think much of Freddie, either. It would have been better if they'd both gone into that hole and never climbed out. Still, at least Donald won't be resting in peace. He carried too much guilt. Not like me. Even though..."

I lifted my gaze from the vicious ads slandering Donald's business. "Even though what?"

"I feel a touch of guilt. Mainly pride, but it wasn't the kindest thing to do." Clifford shrugged, a mischievous smile on his face.

"What do you feel guilty about?"

He chuckled and pressed a finger to his lips. "Nothing."

"Go on, what did you do?"

Clifford took his time sipping from his mug. "I didn't kill Donald, if that's what you're thinking, but I was angry with him. He ruined my dreams. And I was angry with myself for letting him. So I had some fun and left notes on his car. I'd watch as he read them and get incensed. It made my day."

"Oh! You left those threatening notes?"

"They weren't threatening. Well, maybe a bit. They drove him crazy. And he blamed his wife for them. Those two were so wrong for each other, and they'd find any excuse to argue."

"Clifford, this isn't a joke. The police believe Brittany left those notes, and she's considered the prime suspect, even though I know she didn't do it."

His eyebrows danced up and down, and his forehead wrinkles deepened. "How do you know she's innocent? Brittany is crazy enough to kill."

"It's how I got involved in this case. I'm Brittany's alibi. Despite that, the police are still looking at her for the crime."

"Huh! That's unfortunate. I didn't know she was in the frame. The woman has always been unbalanced, but I wouldn't like her to go down for something she didn't do." Clifford leaned forward, his brandy breath huffing over me. "You're certain she didn't do it?"

"Certain. You must tell the police you left those notes. Otherwise, Brittany is in trouble."

"I'll speak to them and make them see sense. But they'd better not pin it on me if Brittany is out of the picture." His laughter died when I didn't smile. "Is that really why you're here? You think I killed Donald?"

I didn't feel under threat from Clifford. I felt sorry for him. He'd been badly treated by someone he trusted, so I understood his anger. "I don't think you're a murderer. But I want to find out what happened to Donald. A murder so close to home is shocking, especially when I feel involved."

He regarded me for several silent seconds. "You didn't do it, did you?"

"I definitely didn't. And neither did Brittany."

"So you thought the jaded business partner committed the dark deed?" Clifford shook his head and raised his flask. "I'll admit, I had a long-held grudge against Donald. I'll also admit to leaving the notes, maybe even scratching my keys along his hearse now and again. And I see why you think I'd be involved. I've got a great motive, haven't I?"

"You have."

"But you still think I'm not guilty. Why?"

"Don't take this the wrong way, but you're not strong enough to... deal with Donald in that way."

"Shove him in a grave and hurl a giant stone on his nasty little head. You're right about that. If I'd killed him, and I've thought about this, I'd have run him over in a hearse. Those things would fell a hippo." Darkness tinged his quiet laugh. "You're right, though. I'm a broken husk of a man. Good for nothing."

"I didn't mean that—"

"I did." He emptied his flask. "I was here. And as you can see, I like a drink. I let it get the better of me. When Donald was discovered, I was asleep. Well, passed out drunk and snoring."

"Can anyone vouch for that?"

"Lots of people. They do afternoon yoga, too. On the day of the delightful murder, I'd had one or two or three brandies and wandered outside. They left the yoga mats out, so I settled on one and had forty winks. The warden woke me, and there were half a dozen people looking at me." He rubbed the back of his neck. "Ask anyone, and they'll happily tell you the story of drunken Clifford and how he snores like a bulldog."

A phone rang inside the bungalow.

Clifford heaved himself out of his seat. "I've been expecting a call from my physio. Can't get this back pain to shift, no matter how much I get pummeled and cracked."

"Thanks for talking to me. I need to get back and open my café. I'll see myself out."

He raised a hand as he shuffled away. "Come back any time. It's nice to have the company. And the food."

I tidied the breakfast things, left the remaining treats in the kitchen for Clifford to enjoy, and left with Meatball. I was walking along the path when the warden stepped out of another property.

"Had a good breakfast?" she asked.

"Yes, thanks." I glanced over my shoulder. "Can I ask, did Clifford drink too much and pass out on the yoga mats recently?"

The warden cast her eyes to the sky. "I don't know why he's so proud of telling everyone that. It's becoming a regular thing, though, and I'm worried about his drinking. He's done it three times in the last week. If he's not passed out drunk in the flower beds, he's sleeping it off inside. I know he's had a troubled past, but this can't go on."

"Um... I eat when stressed. People have different ways of coping."

"Clifford needs to find better coping mechanisms, or he'll end up in a grave like his former business partner. If you'll excuse me." The warden bustled along the path.

I hurried along behind her. "You know about the murder?"

"Bad news travels fast. And Clifford was mumbling during his last drinking session. Something about karma and justice. I don't often listen to his drunken rambles, but I knew who he was talking about."

"You don't think he was involved?"

She slid me a look of surprise. "Between his dodgy back and fondness for brandy, I'm putting him in the no category for killing Donald."

"Oh! Sure. That makes sense."

The warden slowed. "Watch out for Clifford. Once he's had a few, he'll break out into a rendition of Danny Boy and waltz you around the lawn. I say waltz. It'll be a drunken stumble before you both fall, and I don't need another hip fracture to deal with. Now, I must finish my rounds." She strode away.

I ambled back to the village with Meatball, mulling over everything I'd learned. Clifford wasn't the killer. He was a sick, old man with a drinking problem, and even though he'd been open about his hatred for Donald and had the perfect motive, he wasn't well enough to murder him.

Meatball looked up at me. "Woof?"

"I agree. It wasn't Clifford. But now what? We don't know who killed Donald, and I have to prove Campbell is wrong about Brittany."

Meatball grabbed a stick and wagged his tail.

If only my issues could be as easily solved with a good game of chase stick and a belly rub.

Chapter 12

It had been another quiet morning in the café, which gave me ample time to ponder Donald's murder.

I sat looking out across the street as I ate a homemade quiche and mixed salad for lunch. I'd even snuck Meatball into the café to keep me company. There was no one here, so I wouldn't get complaints.

"How will we solve this, Meatball?" I fed him a small piece of quiche. "It wasn't Brittany, since I'm her alibi. But she has an amazing motive for wanting her awful husband dead."

"Woof!" He wagged his tail in support of Brittany not being the killer.

"I'm certain it wasn't Clifford. He wouldn't have been physically capable because of his drinking problem and back pain. And he was struggling to walk. But again, he has an excellent motive. Being deceived by your best friend and losing all your money would make anyone bitter."

Meatball woofed his agreement again to discount Clifford, although all the pets and treats he got while he was there most likely made him biased.

"That leaves me with Freddie. Again, an excellent motive. They were fierce business rivals. And seeing those poisonous ads Freddie put in the paper is proof he despised Donald. With Donald dead, Freddie has access to all his business."

"Woof, woof!"

"And Freddie had the opportunity. Could he have snuck out of the memorial service, discovered Donald, and killed him?"

Meatball cocked his head and whined, although his attention was on my food and not the twisty murder mystery that had me stumped.

I dug into my quiche before feeding him another piece. "If someone saw Freddie creep out of the church during the service, it could be enough evidence to get Campbell and the police to focus on him rather than Brittany." I sighed. "But what about Freddie's shoulder injury? He's recovering from surgery, so would he have been able to do it? Maybe if he'd been angry enough or barged Donald into the grave with his healthy shoulder. But how did he shove the headstone into the grave to crush Donald?"

Meatball raised a paw.

"It's a mess. But we have to figure this out before Campbell. That annoying man won't defeat me."

The vicar's housekeeper, Mavis, bustled along the street, raising a hand when she saw me. She was headed to the café.

I ate another mouthful of quiche then grabbed my plate and hurried Meatball out the back. He shouldn't have been in the café, but I'd needed a friend to discuss the impossible prospect of solving this murder, and Meatball was the perfect sleuthing sidekick.

I'd just tucked him in his kennel when the front door of the café opened. "Coo-ee! Holly, I need cake."

I washed my hands and hurried to the counter. "What can I get you?"

She beamed at me. "Treats for the vicar. The poor man never rests."

"Happy to help. Although I've seen your Victoria sponge cake, and it's a match for mine."

Mavis blushed with delight. "I've tasted yours, and it's delicious. But I was thinking something different. Something to put a smile on his face."

"He's recently had my cookie crumble cake. Perhaps more of that? It's my cake of the month."

"Perfect." She placed an armful of bagged dry-cleaning on a table as I went to cut a slice of crumble cake. "I'll take the whole thing. His sweet tooth is his one vice. I'll make sure he doesn't eat it in one sitting, though." Mavis patted her stomach. "And he always shares. Such a generous man."

"I'll get you a box. Can you manage it with all that dry-cleaning?"

"Of course. This is just the laundry and mending from the vicarage. It never stops. I thought getting everything spotless would make Reverend Liskard happy, but it's not working." She heaved out a sigh. "Between you and me, since Johnny's wife died, it's reminded the vicar of his own loss."

I set the boxed cake on the counter. "He lost someone recently?"

"His wife died three years ago. Of course, you wouldn't know. You haven't been here that long. It was tragic. She was no age."

"I'm so sorry to hear that. What happened?"

"A stroke. One moment, she was arranging the flowers in the church, and the next, she was gone. Collapsed by the altar. There was nothing they could do to save her."

My hand went to my chest. "That's terrible."

"The vicar doesn't like to talk about it, but he's been spending time with Johnny and helping him with his grief, so it must have brought back memories." Mavis stroked the box. "This cake will cheer him up. And of course, I look after him. I do the cleaning, the cooking, and mend his clothes. Although don't get me started on that mess of candle wax. It took an age to scrape it up and ensure the floor wasn't slippery. He's so clumsy."

"You're good to him." I charged Mavis what it cost to make the cake. She earned little working at the vicarage, and it was for a good cause.

"He even made a mess of his favorite cassock. Tore a piece off and spilled candle wax all over himself. He's lucky he didn't get burned. Typical messy man. What would they do without us?"

I handed her back her change. "He tore his cassock? When was this?"

"I'm not certain. I discovered it after the memorial service we had to remember those lost. He must have been thinking about his wife, not paying attention, and tore a piece off one sleeve. When I asked him about it, he said he caught it on a nail."

My heart picked up. Cassocks were black, and Campbell said there'd been marks on Donald's clothing. Could those marks have been candle wax?

"Don't look so worried. It wouldn't be the first time the vicar's damaged his cassocks. The church is old, and things get broken. Just last month, I caught my hand on a nail poking out of a piece of wood. I had to get a tetanus jab." She pursed her lips. "Maybe he did it when dealing with the smoke alarm. He had to dash off when it blared out during the service."

"There was a fire in the vicarage?"

The café door thumped open, and a nightmare appeared. The fake bailiff stood in the doorway, and she wasn't alone. "Holly Holmes, we're here to collect. And this time, the paperwork is in order, and I have a friend with me. A court appointed bailiff. You're not getting out of paying your debts this time."

Mavis's mouth dropped open, and she flapped her lips like a stranded guppy. "Bailiff! Holly, are you in trouble?"

I rushed around the counter, holding my hands up. "No, you can't come in."

"You don't have your bodyguard to keep us away this time. We're taking what's owed. Move aside, or we'll get the police involved." The woman slapped the paperwork on the counter.

"Come back in half an hour." My gaze shot to Mavis, who watched with bright-eyed interest. I was onto something important relating to Donald's murder, and I couldn't be distracted.

"I should leave." Mavis grabbed the cake. "I need to get to work."

"Wait! What alarm?" I hovered between the debt collectors and Mavis. "I didn't know about a fire."

Mavis was already at the door. "It happened not long after the memorial service started. We had so many people in the church, it was difficult to herd everyone out. The vicar rushed off to deal with the alarm, and I took charge. It took ten minutes before everyone was outside and accounted for. Then I had to check inside the church for stragglers."

I eyeballed the bailiff and her burly companion as they inched closer. "Give me a minute! I'm dealing with a matter of life and death." Or just death. Specifically, a murder.

"Holly, are you okay? You look flushed." Mavis opened the door.

"Was there a fire?" I dashed over and caught hold of her arm.

"Oh, no. Just a foolish prank. Someone deliberately set off the alarm. I hope they're ashamed of themselves for disturbing such a beautiful service." Mavis stared at the bailiff and her companion for a second, then she dashed out. No doubt to tell her friends my café was about to be shut for good.

I turned on my heel and raised my hands to show I wouldn't fight what was about to happen. "Give me half an hour. I can fix this."

"Miss Holmes, we must recover the debt. Give us access to the kitchen, and we'll assess what's in there. Unless you want this matter to go to court. Then you'll have to pay court fees, the loan, and interest."

My head was spinning. I couldn't concentrate on their demands. I'd just figured out who killed Donald. Although I couldn't believe who the killer was.

Meatball rushed out from the back of the café and barked at the bailiff and her companion.

"And I've already warned you about that dog. Get it under control, or I'll have it seized."

"You can't take Meatball and sell him. He's mine."

She smirked. "I didn't mean seized and sold. I meant taken to the pound and destroyed."

I glowered at her then looked out the window. Mavis was hurrying away, and in her haste to escape and spread the gossip, she'd left the clean laundry. And the mending.

My heart skipped a beat. I had a feeling that mending contained a vital clue.

I scooped Meatball into my arms to stop him barking and keep him safe from the glowering debt collectors. Then I took a good look around my beloved café. I couldn't save this, but I could stop a killer.

"Don't cause a mess and shut the door when you leave." I grabbed the laundry Mavis had left behind and raced out the door, tears in my eyes. My dream was over, and my heart hurt thinking about what I'd find when I got back. But I couldn't ignore the information I'd discovered.

I threw the bagged laundry over my shoulder, set Meatball down so he could run beside me, pulled out my phone, and found the number for Audley Castle. As much as Campbell irritated me, I needed backup.

"Good morning, you're through to Audley Castle. How may I help?"

"I need to speak to Campbell Milligan. He's in charge of security. It's urgent."

There was a pause. "Mr. Milligan is on duty."

"Can you patch me through? He wears one of those fancy ear things, doesn't he?"

"I'm sure he does. But he's a busy man. Who's calling?"

I jogged along the street, heading toward the church. "Holly Holmes."

"And what is this regarding?"

"I really must speak to him."

"That's not possible."

"It's about a murder."

There was silence.

"If you can't put me through, give him this message. Tell him it's Holly. Say if the torn cloth was black and the marks on the victim's clothing were candle wax, I know who the killer is."

"I'm sorry?"

"Can you remember that? Tell him those exact words. And let him know I'm heading to the church." I wasn't certain what I'd do when I confronted Reverend Liskard. What if something bad had happened, and he'd accidentally killed Donald? He'd be desperate to confess. There had to be a logical explanation. He was the vicar of our parish. A good man.

"If this is a prank call—"

"It's not. Please, just pass it on. Campbell will understand. Tell him to meet me at the church. I know who did it."

There was another pause. "You said your name is Holly?"

"Yes, I run the café in the village. At least, I did. Just get the information to him."

There was no reply.

"Hello?"

The line was dead.

I stuffed away my phone. "It's just me and you, Meatball."

He gave a joyful bark, enjoying being out and off his leash.

I dashed to the church, my heart pounding in my throat. It must have been an accident. Donald lost his balance and was about to fall into the grave, and the vicar tried to help. That was why his cassock got torn. But what about the headstone? That couldn't have been an accident, too.

My breath shot out of me as I reached the church gate. Reverend Liskard was walking inside with Johnny. He had his arm around the grieving man's shoulders.

I hurried to the church door. As I crept inside, I heard them talking, so hid just inside the main door behind a stone pillar. I needed to get my thoughts in order then figure out how to get the vicar alone so I could talk to him.

"Just stay quiet," Reverend Liskard said. "This'll blow over soon. We're doing the right thing."

Johnny's shoulders were hunched and his head down. "Then why do I feel so bad?"

"He deserved it. We're the righteous."

"I can't stop thinking about it. Donald was a terrible man, but..."

I pressed my lips together. Were they both involved in Donald's murder?

The vicar turned Johnny so he faced him and held onto his shoulders. "Justice had to be done. There was no kindness in Donald, and we've both been on the receiving end of his soulless actions. Now he's dead, he can't hurt anyone else."

Meatball sneezed so loudly he blew hymn sheets off a nearby pew.

Reverend Liskard jumped and looked straight at the spot we were hiding.

I ducked out and raised a hand, trying not to look as guilty as I felt.

"Holly! How long have you been here?" He strode over, Johnny trailing behind him.

I took a step back but then met the vicar's gaze. "I came to talk to you. It seems I need to talk to Johnny, too."

"We're in the middle of something." Reverend Liskard looked at the door.

I wasn't sure whether it was a hint for me to go or a check to see how quickly he could stop me if I tried to escape. "I know what happened when Donald died, but

I'm not completely certain why." I adjusted the laundry over my arm.

"You're not making sense. If you have a private matter to discuss, I can make an appointment to see you later today." Reverend Liskard's forehead shone in the candlelight.

"This won't wait. I wouldn't have put the clues together if it weren't for the wonderful gossip network in Audley St. Mary." I petted Meatball for comfort and to give myself a second to think. "The evidence was all there, though. I just didn't want to believe it when I found the last clues."

"Believe what? Evidence of what?" Reverend Liskard glanced at Johnny, who was staring at me with wide eyes.

"You must have spent a lot of time with Donald," I said. "His work brought him to your church."

"Of course. But I deal with many undertakers." Reverend Liskard came closer. "Holly, what is this about? You seem stressed."

"Discovering who killed Donald would do that to a person."

Johnny closed his eyes and lowered his head.

"I didn't realize you were both involved until now," I said. "Although I figured out you definitely were, Reverend. The torn cassock, the knocked over candles, and the wax on Donald's clothing. The clues point to you."

He forced a laugh and swiped a hand across his forehead. "I'm always tearing my clothing. I'm a klutz."

"You weren't on the day you killed Donald. It wasn't until I learned about the alarm being deliberately set off during the memorial service that I realized you'd done it. You used the fire alarm as a distraction so you could sneak out."

Reverend Liskard said nothing.

"As I ran here, I tried to convince myself it was an accident and maybe he'd fallen into the grave, but you had to make sure he'd never get out by crushing him with a headstone." I rushed out my words, still not believing I was accusing our friendly vicar of murder.

Johnny held his hands together in a prayer position. "I wanted to say something."

"No! We're the righteous." Reverend Liskard turned to Johnny. "You understand."

"I didn't expect you to kill him!"

"Johnny, did you see what happened?" I said. "Did you help?"

"I feel guilty. I told Reverend Liskard of my pain. I'm as guilty as him."

"Enough! It wasn't Johnny. He had nothing to do with this. It was all me." Reverend Liskard stared at the altar, his gaze fixed to a spot on the floor. "I... I have a confession to make."

Chapter 13

I let out a slow breath. I had no clue what to do next. On the TV dramas, the amateur sleuth knew how to handle the big revelation, but I was tongue-tied, sweaty, and close to fainting.

"Let's start at the beginning, shall we?" I placed the laundry on a pew. "I never meant to get involved in figuring out what happened to Donald, but when Brittany dragged me into this situation, I had to see it through to the end."

"And why wouldn't you? You're as good and kind as me. You're the right person to uncover the truth." Reverend Liskard reached for my hand, but I stepped back. "You understand why it was the right thing to do. I look after this parish. I love the people in Audley St. Mary."

"I know that, but murder is wrong. The way Donald treated people made him enemies, but he didn't deserve to die," I said.

"I should have done this a long time ago, but I fought my urge. Despite the man being a thief who preyed on the vulnerable and stole from them when they needed solace, I turned the other cheek. He pushed me to my limit when he exploited me after my wife died. And then what happened with Johnny..." Reverend Liskard looked at the silent, broken man standing close by.

I closed my eyes for a second. "I didn't know Donald cheated you, too. I also didn't know about your wife's sudden death. I'm so sorry about that."

"Thank you. You must understand, this was the only way. It was the only thing that would stop Donald." The vicar paced the aisle, up to the altar, and back again. "When Lauren died so suddenly, I fell apart. Everyone showed me kindness, and I thought Donald had, too. But he presented me with an enormous bill after the funeral. I was stunned. When I questioned him, he pretended it was an error."

"You knew that wasn't the truth?"

"I've seen enough death to know how much it costs. But, of course, grieving people don't question it. They feel cheap for not paying for their loved one's final sendoff." Reverend Liskard's hands repeatedly clenched. "The audacity of the man to think he could get away with deceiving me. I've watched him ever since. And over the years, I discovered an unkind, callous serpent."

"That was a terrible thing for him to do, but you should have involved the police, not murdered him."

Reverend Liskard swung around. "Johnny's wife's wedding ring! He had to sell it to pay for the funeral costs."

I sucked in a breath. "Johnny, is that true?"

He nodded. "I didn't know what a funeral cost. When I got the bill from Donald, I panicked. He said it needed paying in seven days. I only work part-time as a painter and decorator, and I have no savings. I couldn't pay."

My hand went to my jacket pocket, and I pulled out the paint-stained rag Meatball had chased across the churchyard. "Are you sure you didn't help the vicar kill Donald?"

"He didn't. You have my word," Reverend Liskard said. "I'll stand in this church and declare that for the rest of time if I must. I did it. No more innocent people will be harmed because of Donald."

"I wish I had killed him," Johnny said. "But now Donald is dead, I can't stop thinking about it. Was it the right thing to do?"

"Yes! He'd have exploited and hurt more people if I hadn't stopped him."

"I feel responsible," Johnny said to me. "It was the day of the memorial service, and I couldn't stop thinking about my wife. I'd talked to Reverend Liskard about the funeral bill, and he got so angry. I couldn't understand why, but then he told me Donald tried to cheat him, too. That's when I figured it out. I should never have been charged that much. Then I wouldn't have needed to sell Sally's ring."

Reverend Liskard paced the aisle again. "I had to confront Donald and tell him he couldn't keep doing this."

"So you invited him to the church, knowing you'd kill him?" I said.

"No! That was never the plan," Johnny said. "At least, it was never my plan. But I wanted a safe place to talk to him and ask for some of the money back. He laughed at me. I got angry and hit him. We fought, and I knocked over a load of candles. If it weren't for the vicar being there, I... I might have killed Donald. I had my hands around his throat at one point."

"I stopped the fight. Donald was unharmed. Johnny deserves no punishment," Reverend Liskard said.

"That's how the candle wax got on the floor," I said, "and on Donald's clothing."

"I didn't even notice the candles in the chaos," Reverend Liskard said. "But I heard everything Donald said to Johnny. It brought back memories of his attempted deception. I knew then I was being shown the right path. I had to stop this devil."

"You knew Donald would be at the open grave during the memorial service?" I said.

"I made a point of asking him to be there at a particular time because the family had concerns about costs and had to talk to him." Reverend Liskard shook his head. "Donald never missed a chance to make more money and convince someone his outrageous fees were worth it."

"Donald was waiting by the grave, and once everyone was inside the church, you set off the smoke alarm, giving yourself a chance to get out and kill Donald without being seen," I said. "And then you discovered the body. You were so convincing when I talked to you about it."

The vicar sighed. "I have an excellent poker face. It comes from years of hearing other people's dark secrets and not reacting. Donald resisted me when I shoved him. He grabbed me and tried to take me in with him."

"Which is how your cassock got torn. Donald had a piece of cloth in his hand from his killer's clothing." My gaze went to the laundry. I'd just brought that evidence with me. Evidence that needed to be with the police.

"I set off the alarm," Johnny said.

"Because I asked you to." Reverend Liskard stared hard at me. "That was Johnny's only involvement."

"But you knew what the vicar had planned?" I said to Johnny. "You went along with it, anyway?"

"I thought I'd feel better after Donald was dead, but I feel awful. We shouldn't have done it."

"You did nothing wrong. And neither did I," Reverend Liskard said. "Holly understands that. Donald was about to cheat her, too. I saw the bill for Sally's wake, and it was reasonable. Of course, Donald knew you were new to the catering business and thought you'd be an easy target. He was a bad man. The world won't miss him."

I couldn't disagree with that. But I could disagree with murder, no matter the motive.

"Holly, you can't tell anyone. Only the three of us know. Who'd benefit from having a cherished vicar taken from this parish? I look after the elderly, the lonely, and the sick. I even support your business when funds allow. I did a service to the community by destroying Donald."

For the briefest second, I was conflicted, but then I shook my head. "There's never a good enough reason for murder."

Reverend Liskard strode closer. Meatball growled and stood in front of me, making the vicar slow.

I backed to the door, Meatball my furry, protective shadow. "It's wrong to hide this."

"I serve the community! And I served them by murdering Donald." He grabbed my wrist. "Do the right thing."

Meatball bounced around, nipping at the vicar's ankles and snarling.

I tugged against Reverend Liskard's strong grip. "I plan to. I can't let you get away with this. Now, let me go."

"Johnny, help me. We can't let Holly go to the police. She'll ruin everything. We could both go to prison."

Johnny's mouth was open, but his gaze was behind me.

I looked over my shoulder, and there was Campbell. "Don't just stand there, help!"

He marched over, a scowl on his face. "Let her go, Reverend Liskard. I heard everything. You're under arrest for murder."

***

I sat on the side of the road, my knees up and my arms wrapped around them.

Meatball sat beside me, occasionally hopping up and licking the tears off my cheeks. By the time I'd confronted Reverend Liskard, and Campbell had taken him and Johnny away, it was too late to save my café.

When I'd returned, the place had been cleared out. Everything I needed to run the business was gone.

They'd even eaten some of my cake, too. That hadn't been paid for.

Meatball nuzzled his nose into my lap, and I scratched between his ears. My heart was broken. Everything I'd worked so hard for had been taken.

My dream was over, my business gone, and at the end of the month, I'd be thrown out of my apartment above the café.

Only Meatball's comforting presence stopped my heart from completely shattering. "At least I've got you. And I'll always find enough money to make sure you never run out of treats."

He licked my cheek again.

"Hey, I thought you might need this." Brittany approached, holding out a takeout mug. "I saw your stuff being taken. Is it true, it was bailiffs?"

I nodded. "I let a few bills get on top of me, and I couldn't compete with your low prices."

She hitched up her leather skirt and sat beside me. "I heard you left the bailiff in the café to confront the vicar. Did he really kill Donald?"

I let out a sigh and looked in the takeout mug. A pale, weak tea stared back at me. I put the lid back on and set it to one side. "I see the gossip mill is operating like an oily otter slipping down a slide."

Brittany shook her head. "You know my feelings about village gossip. Although at least this means people will stop talking about me as if I'm the black widow of Audley St. Mary's. But the vicar! Talk about a shocker. It makes me want to pack up and leave."

"Donald's cheating ways caught up with him," I said. "He tried to con the vicar out of money after his wife's death, and when he did the same to Johnny, Reverend Liskard snapped. He got rid of Donald to make sure he couldn't hurt or con anyone else."

She blew out a breath. "That's why I never trust a man. He could be in a suit or a dog collar, but you can guarantee there's always something shady going on.

That was why I got so obsessed with Donald. I knew he was up to no good. I had to find out what he was sneaking around and doing behind my back."

I glanced at her. "You don't seem all that sad or angry. I thought you loved Donald."

"Well, I've been thinking. Donald *was* a scumbag. He messed with me, he messed with his business partners, and he cheated people. Still, we're married, and I know what's in his will. I'm getting it all. Thanks for figuring it out, Holly." She patted my knee, stood, and strolled back to her café.

I glowered at her retreating form. I should never have given her an alibi. If Brittany had been put away for murdering Donald, I'd still have a business, and her horrible café would be shut.

My gaze settled on the crowd across the road in Café Costel. It wasn't such a horrible place, but I was allowed to feel sorry for myself. I'd lost everything, and Brittany had landed on her high-heeled feet.

I rested my head on my knees and closed my eyes.

"You should be careful loitering. You'll get run over."

I jerked up my head and discovered a smart black SUV parked on the other side of the road. Campbell was walking toward me.

"That's not the way I'd say thank you for figuring out who killed Donald," I said.

He held out a hand. "Holmes, you're a mess."

I grasped his hand, and he pulled me up so hard I thought I'd gotten whiplash. "Thanks for noticing."

"I heard the debt collector came back with the right paperwork and backup."

"Not much gets past you, other than a killer."

Campbell took off his sunglasses and narrowed his eyes. "We were almost there."

"Or you would have been if you'd stopped focusing on Brittany." I glared at her café. "Since you owe me, any chance you could find some health violation or rule break that means she has to close?"

He smirked. "That's outside my remit. Unless Brittany directly threatens the Audley family, you're on your own with that problem."

"I should have said that to you, instead of figuring out what happened to Donald."

"I didn't need you to figure anything out. I strongly suggested you keep your nose out of this murder several times."

"I had to stop a killer." And prove a tiny point to Campbell that he wasn't an unstoppable super-agent who had all the answers.

Campbell sighed. "You did the right thing, even though it was foolish and you could have gotten killed."

"Stopping the bad guy and getting justice is never foolish, even if the person he killed wasn't a nice man."

"I suppose your heart was in the right place. The vicar and his accomplice are talking. They'll be charged any time now."

"Johnny, too?"

"He's involved, but the vicar did the grisly deed."

"You'll charge them yourself?"

"I let the police do the grunt work. They love the paperwork."

I held up a hand to shield my eyes. "The shine from your halo is hurting my eyes."

Campbell kept smirking as he looked at my café. "You're homeless?"

My bottom lip jutted out. "Not yet. The apartment is paid for until the end of the month, so I've got a couple of weeks to figure things out."

"And then?"

I shrugged. "Who knows?"

He put his sunglasses on. "Word has it, Audley Castle kitchen is hiring."

My eyebrows rose. "They are?"

"It's a starter position, so the salary isn't amazing, but you get accommodation thrown in. And they only hire the best." A smile flickered across his face. "You should look into that."

"You want me to work at Audley Castle?"

"Those words didn't come out of my mouth. Personally, I think you're more trouble than you're worth, but Lady Philippa demands you put in an application, and I never ignore a lady's demands. Neither should you. See you around, Holmes." Campbell turned and strode back to the SUV.

I watched the vehicle as the back window slid down. Lady Philippa peered out and finger waved at me as Campbell drove off. I raised my hand, staring along the road long after the SUV had disappeared.

I scooped up Meatball, kissed the top of his head, and smiled. "What do you think? A job at Audley Castle. That could be interesting..."

Also by

Enjoy the complete Holly Holmes cozy culinary
mysteries in paperback or e-book.

Cream Caramel and Murder
Chocolate Swirls and Murder
Vanilla Whip and Murder
Cherry Cream and Murder
Blueberry Blast and Murder
Mocha Cream and Murder
Lemon Drizzle and Murder
Maple Glaze and Murder
Mint Frosting and Murder

Read on for a peek at book two in the series - Cream
Caramel and Murder!

Chapter 1

The chain on the old-fashioned bicycle I rode rattled as I pushed harder. My heart felt like it might burst out of my chest as I leaned over the handlebars. I dug in and eyed the crest of the hill like it was the top prize in a 'win a giant cake' competition.

"Come on, Holly. One small hill won't beat you," I muttered under my breath.

"Woof woof." Meatball turned his head and looked at me from the safety of his basket on the front of the bike.

"That's right. We've done this journey plenty of times. The fact we're pulling what feels like several tons of cake won't defeat us." Cakes I'd lovingly made this morning in the kitchen of Audley Castle.

I puffed out a breath and blew it upward to try to un-stick the sweaty dark hair from my forehead.

I wouldn't slow down or take a break. Mayor Baxter needed his cakes for his afternoon tea party, and I wouldn't let him down.

I lifted a hand and waved as I passed Miss Emily Spixworth's cottage, the door framed by a cascade of beautiful flowering giant pink roses. She stood by the front door, wearing a wide-brimmed hat and gardening gloves, admiring her flowers.

She smiled at me. "Good afternoon, Holly. You've got a load there."

"For the Mayor's party," I said. "I can't stop."

She waved me on. "Have fun."

Fun! Well, I suppose this was a free form of exercise, and using the bike meant I'd never need to join a gym in order to stay fit.

It was one of those ridiculously cute, old-style bikes, with no gears and a wicker basket on the front.

The basket was perfect for Meatball, my beloved dog. As a small corgi cross, he fit perfectly inside. He wore a harness and leash attached to the basket, and a specially designed doggie cycling helmet in a fetching blue, just like mine. Safety first when it came to my favorite little guy.

Meatball loved to go on bike rides with me and was always happy to take in the beautiful sights of Audley St. Mary, where we'd lived for just over a year. He often hung his stubby front paws over the basket and let his ears blow back in the breeze, joy on his furry face as we zoomed about the village.

I made it to the top of the hill and smiled. It was plain sailing all the way down.

We passed a small woodland and flew over the bridge across the river. I still pinched myself most days that I lived in this idyllic, pretty piece of heaven. And I got to live in Audley Castle. How's that for a dream residence?

I slowed the bike as we reached the small parade of shops in the center of Audley St. Mary. I rested my foot on the ground and sighed as I looked at the empty store.

It had once been mine. My own little café. And I'd done well for nine months, tempting people in with my delicious home-made cakes and frothy coffee. It had been a real community hub.

That was until a chain café, which shall not be named and never entered, had opened at the other end of the street.

I'd tried so hard to keep my business going, but I couldn't compete with their special offers and membership discounts. The tourists who frequented the village always went there. It was cheaper, and they recognized the name. They must have been happy to drink weak coffee and eat the stale cakes on offer.

I shook my head. There was no need to be bitter. I'd done my best. The cakes they sold were probably adequate.

"Look, Meatball! It's been sold." I slid off my bike and peered through the soaped over window of the empty store.

"Woof woof." Meatball tilted his tan head from side to side, his ears pricked.

"Yes, it is sad." I patted the window frame like it was my favorite old dog. "Still, we gave it our best shot. And if I still had this café, I wouldn't have taken the job at Audley Castle."

I'd only been working in the kitchens in the castle for three months and was still learning the ropes. The surroundings were beautiful, and most of the staff were amazing, but I'd yet to crack the cool veneer of the strict and imposing Chef Heston. He delighted in yelling at everybody. It was his default setting. The louder he yelled, the harder people worked. That was his theory, anyway.

Although the hours were long, and the pay wasn't amazing, the fact I got to bake every single day more than made up for it. Plus, I got to live in a castle. Well, almost.

Audley Castle was a stunning early seventeenth-century building, designed in a Jacobean style with striking stone cladding. The gardens had been designed by no less than Capability Brown, and there were over a hundred rooms inside and antique furnishings everywhere. It was a beautiful home.

Don't get me wrong, I didn't actually have a room in the castle, but my job came with accommodation set in the beautiful grounds, in a tastefully converted cow shed. It was basic, but it suited Meatball and me just fine.

He whined and leaped up in the basket, resting his paws on the edge. It was a sign he wanted to get out and explore.

"Oh, no. No walk just yet. We've still got these cakes to deliver before we get to have fun." After a final look at my old café, I hopped back on the bike and cycled the last half a mile to Mayor Baxter's elaborate detached house with its thatched roof and wild flower garden.

Climbing off the bike, I hurried along the path to the front door. I knocked, before returning and beginning to unload the cakes from the trolley attached to the back of the bike.

Normally I'd have used the delivery van for such a large amount of cake, but we only had one at the castle at the moment, and Chef had insisted I use the bicycle.

I got the impression he made me use the bike for his own amusement. He told me people liked to have their cakes delivered the old-fashioned way. Apparently, seeing me arrive on a bike reminded them of the old days, when people had time to stop and chat and not race back to their van and hide behind the wheel.

They might, but I had to be extra careful not to bash the cakes around on the journey. And when using the bike, I'd often end up a hot sweaty mess in front of some esteemed members of the local community. That was never a look to aspire to.

Audley St. Mary was a stunning place, and that meant houses came with a hefty price tag and attracted a certain class of people.

"Holly Holmes!" Mayor Baxter stood at the front door as I turned back to the house. "I'm delighted you could bring the cakes."

I hurried back with four carefully balanced boxes of cake in my arms. "Of course. We're always happy to help. Where would you like these?"

"Straight through to the kitchen, same as always." He wore his red mayoral ceremonial robes and his official chains of office around his neck. That meant an important guest was arriving.

I'd been to his house several times to make deliveries and had even convinced him to open my café with a ribbon cutting ceremony. Mayor Baxter was a kind man, a little out of touch at times, but his heart was in the right place.

"How are the Duke and Duchess?" He followed me into the expansive marble and granite kitchen that filled a large extension on the back of the house.

"Both well," I said. The Duke and Duchess of Audley had lived in the castle for decades. It had been their ancestral home for over two-hundred years. They were generous benefactors to the village, ensuring the area flourished under their careful gaze.

"I keep meaning to drop by and take the Duke up on his offer of some trout fishing. The trouble is, I'm so busy entertaining." He patted his round stomach. "Not that I'm complaining. Although I do wish you'd make your cakes a little less delicious. I can never resist a second or even a third helping."

I chuckled as I placed the boxes down. "I'm glad to hear it. I've put some of your favorite caramel cream topped cupcakes in today. Who are you entertaining this afternoon?"

"Three mayors from different counties, their wives, and their assistants. We're talking about setting up a charitable foundation. The trouble is, one of them wants to support farmers, another wants to support wildlife, and I want to help prisoners. I thought, given the work already happening at Audley Castle with your excellent rehabilitation program, it would be a perfect fit. I suspect we'll go around in circles for several meetings before abandoning the project because we can't come to an agreement."

"They all sound like worthy causes," I said. "I'll go grab the last few boxes of cake."

"Right you are." He was already sneaking open one of the boxes and peering inside.

I was mostly self-taught when it came to baking. Although I'd completed two years part-time at a catering college, so I knew how to whip up a good cake.

I also had a love for exploring old recipes and was experimenting with a Roman honey bread that was testing my skills. My last three efforts had been too hard to eat. I was missing a vital ingredient, but I had yet to discover what it was.

I returned with the rest of the cakes to find Mayor Baxter licking his fingers. He grinned when he saw me. "You see, I can never resist your cakes."

"We're always happy to provide cakes for you, Mayor," I said as I set the boxes down.

"Are you busy at the castle today?"

"Always. We've got several coachloads of tourists turning up this afternoon. In fact, I need to get back. There's more baking to do before the end of the day."

"Absolutely! Don't let me keep you." He grabbed a cake out of the box and handed it to me, along with a twenty pound note. "That's for you. For all your hard work."

"Thanks! You don't have to do that." It wasn't uncommon to get tips when I made a delivery, but few were as generous as the mayor. The tips went into my recipe savings pot so I could buy more cook books and maybe take a few courses when I had the time.

"Of course I do. Only the best for the most amazing baker in Audley St. Mary."

I nodded my appreciation as I tucked the tip into my pocket. Some people said Mayor Baxter was on the stuffy side, but he was a nice old guy. He didn't let his position as mayor go to his head and was always happy to chat.

"Thanks again. I'd better get going. Enjoy your tea party."

"No doubt we will." He said goodbye as I headed out the front door and back to the bike where Meatball sat waiting patiently in the wicker basket.

I pushed the bike a short way along the lane and stopped by a bench. I unclipped both our helmets and scooped Meatball out, getting a lick on the cheek as a thank you.

I set him on the ground. "Let's have a ten-minute break before we get back to work."

The journey to Audley Castle would be easy now I wasn't towing the cakes and worrying about hitting a pot hole and sending them flying.

Secretly, I enjoyed the bike rides. It was such a pretty village, and the people were so friendly. I was glad this was my home. Even though my business hadn't worked out the way I'd hoped, I'd landed on my feet by getting the job at Audley Castle.

I bit into the delicious cream caramel frosted cupcake Mayor Baxter had given me and sank back against the seat.

Meatball snuffled around my feet, and I extended his leash so he could wander about and have a good sniff.

I'd gotten Meatball from a rescue center when he was a scraggly sad-eyed puppy. It had been just me and him for a long time. We'd even developed our own language. Well, I say language. I was certain when he barked once, it meant no, when he barked twice, it meant yes, and when he barked all the time, it meant trouble was coming, or to look out because something was happening he was uncertain about.

Some people thought I was crazy for believing I could talk to my dog, but there was something in it, and it worked for us.

I ate my last piece of cake and licked frosting off my fingers before standing. "Time to get back home." I scooped Meatball into my arms and gave him a quick cuddle before settling him back in the basket and attaching our helmets.

I smiled as I turned the bike around. Life was good. Work kept me busy, I was happy with Meatball by my side, and I was making new friends at the castle, including Princess Alice.

Who'd have thought my new best friend would be a princess? She was something like thirty-fifth in line for the throne, so I really was hanging out with royalty.

I sang as I pedaled back toward the castle. Could I sing well? No! But I enjoyed doing it and had no plans to stop if I was in the mood.

Meatball turned, and his eyes narrowed before he started to howl.

I could never be certain if he was happy howling or unhappy howling thanks to my off-key singing.

I laughed as we reached the top of the hill and let my feet slide off the pedals as we freewheeled down, the wind catching my hair and making it fly out behind me.

We shot around a bend, the small woodland on my left a blur of brilliant green. We'd be back at the castle in less than twenty minutes at this rate.

My eyes widened, and I slammed on the brakes as someone stepped out in front of me. The bike skidded, and my breath caught in my throat as I saw who I was about to hit.

"Lord Rupert! Get out the way!" The back wheel lifted off the ground as I was flipped over the handlebars. I flew through the air and landed on top of him.

The bike clattered behind me, and my heart raced as my brain caught up with what had just happened.

I lifted myself off of Lord Rupert, who'd helpfully cushioned my fall. I looked down at his face, and my heart skipped a beat. His eyes were closed.

I'd knocked him out! Or maybe worse.

"Oh my goodness! I'm so sorry." I patted his cheek. "Lord Rupert, are you okay?"

That was a ridiculous question. Lord Rupert Audley, thirty-fourth in line to the throne, had just been jumped on by a ten stone (and a few generous pounds) woman who couldn't control her bike properly.

"Holly! What have you done?" Jenny Delaney rushed out of her cottage opposite the woods, a dishcloth in her hand.

I pushed myself up, my stomach churning as Rupert remained unresponsive. Just how hard had he hit the ground?

"My word!" Jenny peered with wide eyes at the scene. "That's Lord Rupert."

"Um, yes. He just stepped out. I couldn't stop in time." I leaned over him, willing him to be okay.

He didn't stir.

"I'd better call for an ambulance. And the police," Jenny said as she turned back to her cottage. "I think you've killed him!"

***

Cream Caramel and Murder is available to buy in paperback or e-book format.

Inspiration

A single visit to a grand historic home in England sparked the idea for the Holly Holmes series.

Audley End House's history traces back to its origins as Walden Abbey, a Benedictine monastery founded in the early 12th century. During the Dissolution of the Monasteries in the 16th century, King Henry VIII seized the abbey's lands. It was then granted to Sir Thomas Audley, who later became Lord Chancellor of England. Audley demolished much of the abbey and began building a new mansion on the site in 1603. The mansion passed through various owners over the centuries, each leaving their mark on the estate through renovations, expansions, and enhancements.

A day trip to see this impressive mansion led me on a three-year journey with Holly, Meatball, and the fictional Audley family.

I was wowed by the architecture, which is a blend of original Jacobean mansion, built by Thomas Howard, the Palladian style designed in the 18th century by the Braybrooke family. The Great Hall is a notable feature, with its soaring ceilings, intricate woodwork, and impressive fireplace. The State Apartments are adorned with fine furnishings, tapestries, and artwork, reflecting the tastes of its former inhabitants. The exterior of the mansion boasts imposing facades, ornate stonework, and symmetrical proportions characteristic of Jacobean and Palladian architecture.

As I walked around, all I could think was 'what if a resourceful baker found herself working here and solving crime?'

And although I'm not green-fingered, I have to mention the gardens at Audley End, since several murders take place in the grounds. They're a testament to centuries of meticulous landscaping and design. The extensive grounds encompass formal gardens, woodland walks, and parkland, all meticulously maintained to enhance their natural beauty. The formal gardens feature manicured lawns, flowerbeds bursting with colorful blooms, and classical statuary. The walled kitchen garden is a highlight, supplying fresh produce to the estate and offering visitors a glimpse into historic horticultural practices.

Audley End House and Gardens stand as a testament to England's rich heritage and cultural legacy, inviting visitors to explore, learn, and be inspired by its timeless beauty and historical significance. I was so inspired, I had to write about it.

If you're ever in England and looking for something to do, I highly recommend a visit to this beautiful place.

Recipes

Enjoy this selection of delicious recipes, all with a yummy cookie theme!

Meatball and Princess Alice approved.

Classic Chewy Chocolate Chip Cookies

These cookies are bursting with melty chocolate chips and have a perfect balance between crisp edges and a soft, chewy centre.

Prep time: 15 mins   **Cooking time:** 10-12 mins

This recipe yields 12 large cookies.

Ingredients:

225 grams (1 cup or 2 sticks) unsalted butter, softened
200 grams (1 cup) light brown sugar
100 grams (½ cup) granulated sugar
2 large eggs
2 teaspoons pure vanilla extract
280 grams (2 ¾ cups) all-purpose flour
5 ml (1 teaspoon) baking soda
5 ml (1 teaspoon) salt
400 grams (2 cups) semisweet chocolate chips

Instructions:

1. Preheat oven to 375°F (190°C) and line baking sheets with parchment paper.

2. In a large bowl, cream together the softened butter and sugars until light and fluffy. Beat in the eggs one at a time, then stir in the vanilla extract.

3. In a separate bowl, whisk together the flour, baking soda, and salt. Gradually add the dry ingredients to the wet ingredients, mixing until just combined. Don't overmix!

4. Fold in the chocolate chips with a spatula.

5. Scoop heaping tablespoons of dough and roll them into balls. Place the dough balls on the prepared baking sheets, leaving a few inches between each cookie for spreading.

6. Bake for 10-12 minutes, or until the edges are golden brown and the centers are slightly soft. Let the cookies cool on the baking sheet for a few minutes before transferring them to a wire rack to cool completely.

Tips:
- For chewier cookies, use mostly brown sugar. For crispier cookies, use more white sugar.

- Chilling the dough for at least 30 minutes before baking helps prevent the cookies spreading.

- Sprinkle sea salt on top of the cookie dough balls before baking for a sweet and salty flavor explosion.

Chocolate Chip Cookie Bars

Imagine sinking your teeth into a decadent slice of heaven. Oozing with melted chocolate and boasting a perfect balance of sweetness and richness.

Picture yourself savoring them on a lazy Sunday afternoon, accompanied by a steaming cup of coffee or a tall glass of cold milk. Their irresistible aroma fills the kitchen, beckoning everyone within sniffing distance to gather round and indulge.

Prep time: 20 minutes   **Bake time:** 25 minutes

Makes up to 24 small bars or 12 large bars

Ingredients:
1 cup (2 sticks / 226g) unsalted butter, melted
1 cup (200g) brown sugar
1/2 cup (100g) granulated sugar
2 large eggs
2 teaspoons (10ml) vanilla extract
2 cups (250g) all-purpose flour
1 teaspoon (5g) baking soda
1/2 teaspoon (2.5g) salt
1 1/2 cups (270g) chocolate chips

Instructions:

1. Preheat oven to 350°F (175°C). Grease a 9x13-inch baking dish.

2. In a large bowl, mix melted butter, brown sugar, and granulated sugar until well combined.

3. Beat in eggs and vanilla until smooth.

4. Stir in flour, baking soda, and salt until just combined.

5. Fold in chocolate chips.

6. Spread the batter evenly into the prepared baking dish.

7. Bake for 25-30 minutes or until golden brown and a toothpick inserted into the center comes out clean.

8. Allow to cool before cutting into bars.

Oreo Truffles

Indulge in a heavenly treat that's easy and irresistible. Luscious spheres of velvety Oreo goodness, encased in a blanket of rich, melted chocolate. With three simple ingredients, you'll embark on a journey of decadence that will have everyone clamoring for more.

Prep time: 15 minutes   **Freeze time:** 30 minutes

Makes 36 small truffles.

Ingredients:
1 package (about 36) Oreo cookies
1 package (8 ounces) cream cheese, softened
12 ounces chocolate chips, melted

Instructions:
1. Crush the Oreo cookies into fine crumbs using a food processor or by placing them in a sealed plastic bag and crushing them with a rolling pin.

2. In a mixing bowl, combine the Oreo crumbs with softened cream cheese until well blended.

3. Roll the mixture into small balls and place them on a parchment-lined baking sheet.

4. Freeze the balls for about 30 minutes.

5. Dip each frozen ball into the melted chocolate to coat completely.

6. Place the coated balls back onto the parchment-lined baking sheet.

7. Refrigerate until firm, about 1 hour.

Peanut Butter Blossom Cookies

These Peanut Butter Blossom Cookies are a delightful mix of sweet, nutty peanut butter and rich chocolate, making them a beloved classic for any occasion. Enjoy baking and indulging in these irresistible treats!

Prep time: 20 minutes   **Bake time:** 10 minutes

Makes 36 small cookies

Ingredients:
1/2 cup (100g) granulated sugar
1/2 cup (100g) packed brown sugar
1/2 cup (125g) creamy peanut butter
1/4 cup (57g) unsalted butter, softened
1 egg
1 1/4 cups (156g) all-purpose flour
1/2 teaspoon (2.5g) baking powder
1/2 teaspoon (2.5g) baking soda
36 chocolate kisses, unwrapped

Instructions:

1. Preheat oven to 375°F (190°C). Line baking sheets with parchment paper.

2. In a large mixing bowl, cream together granulated sugar, brown sugar, peanut butter, butter, and egg until smooth.

3. In a separate bowl, combine flour, baking powder, and baking soda.

4. Gradually add dry ingredients to the creamed mixture, mixing well after each addition.

5. Shape dough into 1-inch balls and roll them in granulated sugar.

6. Place balls 2 inches apart on prepared baking sheets.

7. Bake for 8-10 minutes or until lightly golden.

8. Immediately press a chocolate kiss into the center of each cookie.

9. Cool on baking sheets for 5 minutes before transferring to wire racks to cool completely.

Cookie Dough Ice Cream Cake

Indulge in a delightful union of creamy ice cream and irresistible cookie dough in this decadent treat. Layers of velvety vanilla ice cream are interspersed with chunks of edible cookie dough, nestled atop a buttery cookie crust. This frozen masterpiece is the ultimate treat for any occasion.

Prep time: 20 minutes   **Freeze time:** 4 hours

Ingredients:
1 1/2 cups (150g) cookie crumbs (crushed cookies)
1/3 cup (75g) unsalted butter, melted
1 quart (946ml) vanilla ice cream, softened
1 cup (200g) edible cookie dough, divided (store-bought or homemade)

Instructions:
1. In a mixing bowl, combine cookie crumbs and melted butter until well combined.

2. Press the mixture into the bottom of a 9-inch springform pan to form the crust.

3. Spread half of the softened vanilla ice cream

evenly over the crust.

4. Crumble half of the edible cookie dough over the ice cream layer.

5. Repeat with the remaining ice cream and cookie dough.

6. Cover the pan with plastic wrap and freeze for at least 4 hours or until firm.

7. Before serving, run a knife around the edges of the pan to loosen the cake, then remove the sides of the springform pan.

8. Slice and serve chilled.

Cookies and Cream Parfait

Treat yourself to a heavenly dessert. Layers of creamy vanilla pudding, crushed chocolate cookies, and fluffy whipped cream. This parfait is sure to satisfy your sweet cravings and leave you longing for just one more bite.

Prep time: 25 minutes (including chilling time)

Ingredients:
1 package (3.4 ounces/96g) instant vanilla pudding mix
2 cups (473ml) cold milk
1 cup (100g) chocolate sandwich cookies, crushed
1 cup (240ml) heavy cream
2 tablespoons (25g) granulated sugar
1 teaspoon (5ml) vanilla extract

Instructions:
1. In a mixing bowl, whisk together the instant vanilla pudding mix and cold milk until smooth and thickened. Refrigerate for 5-10 minutes to set.

2. In serving glasses or bowls, layer the crushed chocolate sandwich cookies and prepared vanilla pudding, alternating between the two

until the glasses are filled.

3. In a separate mixing bowl, whip the heavy cream, granulated sugar, and vanilla extract until stiff peaks form.

4. Spoon a generous dollop of whipped cream on top of each parfait.

5. Garnish with additional cookie crumbs, if desired.

6. Serve your parfaits chilled.

About the author

K.E. O'Connor (Karen) is a cozy mystery author living in the beautiful British countryside. She loves all things mystery, animals, and cake.

When she's not writing about mysteries, murder, and treats, she volunteers at a local animal sanctuary, reads a ton of books, binge-watches mystery series on TV, and dreams about living somewhere warmer.

To stay in touch with the fun, clean mysteries, where the killer always gets their just desserts and receive a free novella featuring Holly and Princess Alice:

Newsletter: https://BookHip.com/SQZPPHC
Website: www.keoconnor.com
Facebook: www.facebook.com/keoconnorauthor

Made in the USA
Middletown, DE
08 June 2024

55499047R00092